CH00642323

CLAIMED

THE DANGEROUS BILLIONAIRE
JASPER BLACKSTONE

Z.L. ARKADIE

Copyright © 2019 by Flaming Hearts Press LLC

All rights reserved.

No part of this book may be reproduced in any form or by any electronic or mechanical means, including information storage and retrieval systems, without written permission from the author, except for the use of brief quotations in a book review.

ISBN: 978-1-942857-51-8

CONTENTS

AUTHOR'S NOTE

As of May 7, 2022, this book has been updated. The POV is now first-person present tense to improve readability and pacing. Also, story elements have been refined.

If you read the original version of Desire, you'll find that some story elements that are to payoff in Claimed no longer exist. The original version chased down way too many plot lines. For instance, the entire Rochester report double cross plot has been cut. Also, the BFE sexual misconduct storyline isn't in the revised version. A different inciting incident occurs that brings us to the start of Claimed (Book 3). But the main plot points are the same. A major reason for the revision is that there were way too many plot lines for one trilogy.

Also, as of August 15, 2022, the last name of the main family has been changed from Christmas to Blackstone.

I hope you enjoy!

ONE

THE THIRD TRIPLET
HOLLY HENDERSON

It feels as if the wide-open space of the grocery store is caving in on me. My head feels floaty as I split my attention between Jasper and the checkout clerk, who is a dead ringer for Bryn Blackstone. Trapped in indecision, I focus on Jasper's voice. He says my name again. The caution in his tone implies that he doesn't want me to be reckless. He sees her too. I wonder why his jaw hasn't hit the floor.

But I set my focus back on the woman working the cash register. Her skin has turned red and blotchy, I think she's trying not to look in my direction while passing grocery items over the scanner. But I can't take my eyes off her. Suddenly, her glower meets my gaze as she waits for the customer to complete the transaction on the keypad. Very quickly, I'm able to see noticeable differences between her and Bryn. She's slender but not as frail as Bryn. Her hair color and style are remarkably similar to Bryn's, but the cashier's loose curls are about two inches longer. The young woman wears a diamond stud in her nose. Bryn doesn't.

"Holly," Jasper says, this time louder. I look up at him standing beside me with his mouth open. "Let's talk."

His breath wafts over my face and his familiar scent instantly makes me feel close to him again. I can't believe my heart, betraying me this way. Well, my mind won't have it. Regardless, his closeness acts as a powerful agent against my determination to immediately address the woman at the cash register and find out why she's a dead ringer for Jasper's sister and my friend.

Jasper takes my shopping cart by the handle and then turns to the woman behind me. "Excuse us."

The woman bats her eyelashes as if he's just breathed charm dust on her. "Sure, darling."

Bryn's counterpart, who I'm sure is Eve, watches Jasper and me as she rings up groceries. She looks as if the fact that I said her name hasn't quite fully sunk in, although she's slowly coming to some sort of awareness that I'm in the Long Island grocery store because I'm looking for her. Anxiety flutters in my chest as I walk beside Jasper while he pushes my cart down an aisle. His large hand is wrapped securely around my waist. I don't know if I'm doing the right thing by taking my eyes off my mark. But what's she going to do, escape in the middle of her shift? I hope not. We turn down an empty aisle where the spaghetti sauces and other like products are shelved.

When we're out of everyone's sight, I snatch myself out of his hold. "What are you doing here?" Even though I'm spitting fire, I make sure I keep my voice low. Truth be told, I'm happy to see him. He needs to be here for this. I point toward the registers. "Did you see that? She looks like Bryn. We can't let her get away." I take a step around Jasper.

Once again, he hooks me by the waist. "Babe, you're making a scene."

Babe? I frown and take stock of all the emotions that are swirling inside me. My anxiety, pain, and anger—especially anger—are suddenly overriding my fretting about the cashier.

"You never answered me. What the hell are you doing here, Jasper?" I snap, snarling.

He opens his mouth to speak, but I have more to say. "Because I've seen the pictures of you and Julia, and you look like the real thing to me and then yesterday I saw you two together." My thoughts are coming too fast. "Then your future father-in-law showed up at my suite and threatened my life." I slap my chest. "No, not my life—he threatened *your* life."

Quickly, he pulls me closer, reminding me that I am indeed in his arms. "My future father-in-law?" He seems to be trying to figure out whoever could that be. And then his eyes burst wide before they frown again. "Are you talking about Valentine?"

"Yes," I sound and feel like I'm out of breath.

"He did what?"

I shrink in his arms as I try to figure out how to answer his question. I surely do not want Jasper to storm out of the store to go beat Arthur Valentine to a pulp. But that has more to do with Jasper's safety than Valentine's well-being.

"Forget it," I say. "It doesn't matter. He wants me to leave you alone. You've already decided that for us."

His glare makes me dizzy—so intense, so deep. "Did Arthur himself go to your room?"

I look impatiently towards the front of the store. I nod.

His face tightens as his chin floats upward. "Did he touch you?" He sounds pained.

The memory of Valentine's goon grinding his

erection against my ass makes me want to vomit. I squeeze my eyes shut to forget it.

"I'm going to kill him," Jasper says through clenched teeth.

I didn't mean to anger him, so I soften my gaze as much as I can. "He didn't hurt me, Jasper. I'm fine. Just let it be. I don't want you in prison for murder."

His blinking increases, as though he's processing my words. The look on his face, I can tell Jasper is not going to let it be.

"Plus, I have a more pressing issue facing me. Did you see her? The Bryn look-alike?" I ask, pointing to the front of the store. I need him to fucking focus on what's really important at the moment.

His lips press together tightly, but slowly, the tension eases from his mouth. "Yes, I saw her. Who is she?"

"Her name is Eve." I frown. "I think. And I can't lose her right now." I thumbed over my shoulder. "So I have to go. Maybe I'll talk to you later, maybe not."

He snorts as if I'm talking foolishly. "We're doing this together."

I tap myself on the chest. "This is my thing, not yours."

"She resembles my sister, so this is more my thing than it is yours."

I scoff. "I'm not leaving her in your hands, Jasper."

His head flinches back. "What the hell do you mean by that?"

"If I leave her in your hands, she might get lost in the deep dark cemetery of the Hudson Bay or something."

He quickly closes the distance between us and now we're standing face to face, our breaths crashing into each other. "Is that what you think of me—that I would murder an innocent woman?"

My anger betrays me by melting away because I've offended him and feel awful about it. "I don't know what I think of you," I say flatly.

His lips part as he stares into my eyes. It's as though we are the only two people in the entire supermarket. I can tell he wants to kiss me, but something is holding him back.

Jasper's breaths tremble, and then he clears his throat. "Her name is Eve?" he whispers.

I pull my eyebrows then release them. "Yes."

"Is she the result of your trip to Chattanooga?"

I nod.

"Let me talk to her, and you stay close," he says.

Suddenly, I'm struck by a thought. "You said my name."

He grimaces. "What?"

"You called me Holly. If she's Eve, then she knows who I am." I bolt down the aisle. Eve had warned me to leave her alone, and now she knows I'm here. Jasper had tipped her when he called my name.

Jasper matches me step for step until his powerful figure sweeps past me. The number of shoppers in the store seems to have doubled, and all the new bodies are in the way. My eyes find what I think is the same cash register Eve had been working, but another girl is ringing up groceries at that station. Jasper steps past me and searches the next line and then the next. Finally, we look at each other in defeat. Eve has escaped us.

TWO
FINDING EVE
HOLLY HENDERSON

The manager, standing behind a station at the front of the grocery store, looks irritated by the question I just asked him. "Eve?" Interesting, he doesn't recognize the name.

"The cashier who was at that register." I point to the register Eve had abandoned.

His frown grows more intense. "Faye?"

"Yes, Faye," I say.

"She wasn't feeling well and..."

My chest tightens. That's all I need to hear before I'm running toward the glass doors, squinting at the parking lot, looking for moving vehicles. Now that I'm outside, the cold squeezes the living daylights out of me as snow flurries blast my face. I finish scanning the parking lot. A few cars drive in and out at careful speeds, I would think if Eve or Faye is behind the wheel, her car would go skidding into the streets.

So quickly the outside temperature quells the body heat my running generated. "I think she's gone," I whisper to myself.

"Do you have her home address?" Jasper asks.

I jump startled, too trapped in my own crisis to realize he's standing beside me. I don't want to answer his question, but if I play this all wrong, I fear I won't be able to get rid of him. He should definitely not be around when I interview Eve to find out what she's so afraid of. I need to be careful about what I say next.

"Yeah, I have it. I'll have my Lyft driver take me to her place." I pat his arm like we're old friends—*gosh it feels so good to touch him.* "If I hear anything, I'll call you."

"I sent your driver away," Jasper says as if it's no big deal.

I stare at him incredulously, suddenly caught between a rock and a hard place. "Why would you do that?"

He nods casually at an SUV blowing plumes of smoke out of the tailpipes. "You're safer with me. Come on."

His hand is on my back, beckoning me to move fast. I want to brat-out, yell at him and tell him, "Fuck you, fuck you, fuck you!" But there's not a stitch of time for tantrums. If I don't want to lose Eve again, then I better get to her fast. But I hope Jasper doesn't think he's running this show because he's not —I am.

I'm working, and not only is he in my way but he's made things astronomically harder for me by sending away my car and driver. So, if I apply common sense, I can't tell him to go back to his office and fiancé. I need him. *Shit!* I need him.

THE INSIDE of Jasper's car smells like brand new leather mixed with the subtle scent of his delicious cologne. As soon as we're inside I give him the address and he plugs it into the navigator. I shiver slightly as he drives quickly but cautiously across the snow-covered roads.

Even though the car is comfortably warm, my fingers haven't thawed quite yet. I shove my hands into my coat pocket and let my teeth clatter as I sip in temperate air.

Jasper's long arm reaches out and turns up the heat.

I should say thank you even if I'm mad at him for undermining my investigation. "Thank you," I whisper, turning to watch the town pass by my window.

The soft leather beneath Jasper squeaks, signaling that he's shifting in his seat. "Holly, you mentioned photos. What photos were you talking about?" he asks.

Gas stations and storefronts pass by but I can't seem to focus on the activity going on beyond my window as memories of the pictures of Jasper and Julia together shuffle through my head.

"Pictures of you and Julia." The most disturbing photo freeze-frames in my mind. "You even traveled to the desert together." My voice cracks.

"What?" He sounds either impatient or flabbergasted, maybe both.

I quickly turn to face him. His eyebrows are pinched as he splits his attention between me and the road, waiting for me to elaborate.

I tell him about how Rachel and Kylie showed me the photos yesterday morning. They were mostly a series of selfies with him and Julia looking like an engaged, attractive, and perfectly content couple.

He laughs with an edge when he declares, "I've

never taken a selfie in my life, let alone taken one with Julia."

The fact that Jasper is still referring to me as 'babe' doesn't go unnoticed. Also, I believe him.

"Then where do you think they came from?" I ask.

"Julia is the obvious suspect. It's something she'd spend her time doing."

Now, in my mind's eye, I see them walking out of that building together. "But the way you touched her yesterday..." I say, shaking my head continuously.

He's frowning again. "Touched her like what?"

"With your hand on the small of her back, like she belongs to you."

"Julia does not belong to me, Holly." His eyes caress me lovingly during the glance that he steals at me. "You do."

Tears fill my eyes and my heart wants to weep with relief. I feel his claim through and through. However, he's still linked to the Valentines. It's that fact alone that has made me so insecure, and I'm never insecure.

Somehow, I'm able to keep my tears from spilling out. I swallow to clear my throat. At least now I don't want to punch his lights out anymore.

"By the way, how were you able to find me?" I ask in a small voice.

Jasper steels a glance at me as the navigator tells him to make the next right. He rubs his jaw as if uncomfortable about what he's going to say next.

"Understand, Valentine can be a dangerous person." Jasper sounds like he's laying the foundation for a more earth-shattering revelation.

"Don't I know," I say, squeezing my eyes to banish the feel of that man's body against mine.

"I hadn't known he snake his way into your hotel room. I wish you would've called me right away."

I scoff. "So you could kill him?"

"No. Death is an easy way out. You have to be alive to feel the pain."

I look at him incredulously. He said that with such ease and so matter-of-fact. Sometimes I get a glimpse of the Jasper that you definitely don't want to fuck with, and I just saw him. I'm not intimidated by him or his evil twin, though. Perhaps it's because I know neither will ever 'torture' me.

That's why I continue pushing for a satisfactory answer. "But how did you find me all the way in Long Island?"

He makes a sound when he sighs like he's uncomfortable about telling me the truth.

"Don't worry, Jasper," I say with a soft and nervous laugh. "I wouldn't be surprised if you stuck a tracking chip in my skin while I was sleeping. Anyone who has your kind of control issues would do something like that."

He's not amused by my joke. But there's something in the pause that alarms me.

My mouth falls open. "You put a tracking chip in my skin?"

Jasper's Adam's apple bobs as he swallows hard.

"Open your purse, unzip the part where you keep coins, and search through your loose change."

Frowning, I open and do as instructed. I don't keep that much change so it's easy to spot a small round device that resembles a coin cell battery.

I hold up the object, turning it this way and that. "Did you put this in my purse?"

"Yes." It sounds as if he unburdened himself when he admitted that.

The navigator tells him to make a left. Snow flurries pelt the window as he explains how on the night before last, he'd dropped the device into my purse to keep me safe. He knew Valentine saw me as a threat, and had been keeping tabs on the two people Valentine tasked to follow me. He never accounted for

Valentine crawling out of his hole and coming to see me himself.

Jasper rubs the side of his face, which I've learned is something he does when he's deeply thinking. "That's a new one. Valentine likes to keep his hands clean. The fact that he showed up at your suite worries me."

"What's his deal anyway?" I ask. "Forcing marriage to get ahead is so olden days."

"He doesn't want anything to impede me from winning an election. I've always known Arthur to be a man of extremes." Jasper says.

If I weren't strapped into my seat belt, I'd be sitting on the edge of my seat. "What do you mean?"

"He pushes himself from one extreme to the next, never satisfied, and not giving a damn who he destroys along the way—even his son and daughter are not exempt." He steals a glance at me. "He has no conscience, Holly. And he has..." He frowns as if he's reaching deeper inside himself for a more accurate descriptor of his nemesis. "And he has a dark soul."

"So how do you destroy a man who has no conscience and has a dark soul?"

"You seize the source of his power and you never give it back."

My eyebrows are stuck high. He just revealed

how he plans to destroy Arthur Valentine. I have no idea how he's going to do it, but I'm all on board for him trying. I roll the tiny tracker between my fingers. Somehow, Jasper keeping tabs on me to protect me from that kind of person doesn't seem so bad.

"You were right," I finally say. "I thought I could handle Valentine until he..." I squeeze my eyes closed, thinking of his haunting face under the scant glare of light coming from the lamp as he sat in the chair by the window. I try to forget the sound of Valentine's voice warning me. "He said he wouldn't kill me—he'd kill you."

Jasper extends an arm to delicately cup my chin. "That's never going to happen. You can wipe the worry off your conscience."

His hand on my face feels so warm. I want to close my eyes and sink into his touch. But I must continue protecting my heart. I can't let down my guard.

"You're soft," he whispers.

Why haven't I pulled away? My heart knocks like a broken radiator. I'm fighting the urge to take his hand and smash my lips against his palm, kissing him hard. Then his hand abandons my face as he very carefully takes the next turn, following the navigator's direction.

He adjusts hard in his seat, like he's ready to jump out of it. "So... Why does this Eve woman resemble my sister?"

"I don't know yet." I sound winded so I clear my throat. "I mean, I could make an educated guess or two."

"I'd like to hear them." Jasper turns us down a street lined thickly with trees, their branches intermingling dangerously with the power lines.

We're close. I look out the window, searching the driveways of weather-beaten houses. "That she's a third twin."

The SUV slows to stop in front of a Dutch-style home with snow already coating the roof. The navigator's voice says, "Arrived."

And there she is, her shoulder holding the cellphone to her ear as she stuffs a suitcase in the trunk.

"Where is she going?" I whisper.

Jasper and I look at each other incredulously before he pulls up and blocks her car in the driveway. That's when Eve faces us, looking forward as her cellphone drops from her ear and hits the snow-covered pavement.

TOUCHING MY ARM SOOTHINGLY, Jasper beams in on Eve, who reminds me of a deer stuck in the headlights of a quickly approaching car.

"Let me talk to her first," he says.

I shake my head vigorously. "What? No." I say that but I'm not sure if Jasper speaking to Eve first is such a bad thing. She's already rejected talking to me. Maybe a new contact like the half brother she's never met, might shock her enough to make her more malleable.

"Okay," I say, nodding, quickly changing my mind. "Go."

With one hand on the door handle, I sit on the edge of my seat as I watch him say something to her. The soundproofing is remarkable in this SUV. Eve checks over her shoulder as if calculating the distance from where she stands to the confines of her house. Her worried gaze lands on Jasper again. He holds up his hands, showing her he's defenseless. That's my cue, and I take it. I open the door, and step out of the car. The cold air wants to freeze my blood. At least I have her attention, though. She watches me curiously as I close the distance between me and Jasper.

"Eve, it's me—Holly Henderson."

"I told you to leave me alone." She sounds like

she's trying to yell at me but the wind has been knocked out of her.

"Where are you going?" I ask.

She shakes her head stiffly.

"Listen..." Jasper says, and I gently squeeze his arm to silence him. Surprisingly, he adheres to my nonverbal cue.

"Unfortunately, when someone tells me no, that always means yes." I show her a fraction of a smile, but she remains stone-faced. But she folds her arms, which is my cue to keep talking. "I just wanted to have a small conversation with you, but now that I see you're the spitting image of his sister"—I tilt my head towards Jasper—"who's a good friend of mine, naturally, we're beyond curious about who you are. I mean..." I take a few steps toward her, and she doesn't move an inch. That's also a good sign. "Do you know who you are?"

Eve's eyes shift between Jasper and me. "Do I know who I am? What the hell does that mean?"

"Who are your parents?"

Her frown intensifies. "I don't have parents." She's barely audible.

"What about siblings?" I ask quickly in an effort to keep her talking.

She shakes her head.

"I called you Bryn. Have you ever heard of Bryn Blackstone?"

She drops her head, not looking at either of us when she says, "No."

My instincts tell me not to believe her. But why? Does she know who the Blackstones are?

"Bryn is my sister," Jasper finally says. "She's the spitting image of you. But we can get all of this figured out where it's nice and warm. I need you to come with us."

"No," she says, shaking her head adamantly. "I'm not going with you anywhere."

She looks horrified. Even I am looking at him alarmed. I hadn't expected Jasper to say that.

"By the looks of it, you're in hiding," Jasper continues. "Aren't you?"

Eve hesitates. Yet again, she turns to look at the door of her house.

"Do you live alone?" he asks.

Her eyebrows furrow. I think she's wondering if she should answer his question.

"If not, then..."

"Yes," she says like someone who answered one way but suddenly changed their answer.

"Well, Holy here, the woman I love, had a tail on her."

I swallow a gasp as I look at him with wide eyes. He's smiling a little as he continues focusing on Eve though. It's not the part where he said he loves me that startles me. Someone followed me? If so, then how does he know?

He tells her that their father recently died. He was a bad man, who left an enemy he's dealing with in his wake. That man threatened me in my personal space and he's sure to come have someone check into her if he leaves this house without her.

Eve's expression remains unreadable. It's not like she doesn't believe him.

"You know all about bad people, don't you, Eve?" Jasper asks.

After a moment, she closes her eyes gravely and nods.

"For all intents and purposes, I'm your brother, your half brother. Let me protect you."

THREE

CLOSER TO THE TRUTH
HOLLY HENDERSON

Eve sits in the front seat, so Jasper and I can keep an eye on her, and I sit in the back. Jasper is on the phone with his personal assistant, Stephanie. He's spouting giving her a to-do list. The items include making room for one more person on a helicopter that's to take us to an undisclosed location, contacting someone named Dr. Richards to arrange a DNA testing ASAP and preparing a room for Eve. Now Jasper is being briefed by his head of security. I, on the other hand, am ready to test my suspicions. Gina said Randolph used to travel to Chattanooga. I wonder if she's ever seen him. I've already found a picture of Randolph Blackstone that I've been using for research.

I shift to the edge of my seat. "Eve, have you ever seen him?" I show her the picture.

She gasps and slaps a hand over her mouth. "Yes." She's breathless. "That's Arthur."

"Holly, are you wearing your seat belt?" Jasper asks. He sounds irritated.

"No, Eve," I say, ignoring him. "That's Randolph Blackstone. Your father."

"No," she whimpers, shaking her head as if banishing what I revealed from reality. "That man is not my father, no."

"Holly," Jasper snaps.

Eyes closed I sigh hard. I didn't know I would get this reaction from her. Eve is still wiping the tears from her eyes. I pushed too hard, too fast. I should have waited.

It falls silent between us.

"Yes, I'm here," Jasper says to whomever he was speaking to through his earpods.

Neck bent, looking down, out of nowhere Eve says, "My name is Katie. But I prefer Kat."

Jasper glances at me through the rearview mirror. I think I see approval in his eyes.

"But the manager at the grocery store said your name was Faye?"

"It's the name I'm using in this life. But, I've seen

her before, Bryn Blackstone. It was recent. She was on the news as missing. I was with my boyfriend and we were... We were..." Her voice has become shaky. "We couldn't make sense of it."

My head is spinning like crazy. She's thrown a lot at me at once. I have to rationally deduct what's important and what isn't. Eve must be a decoy name that she and Alexia came up with to let her know that her previous life was on her ass. That's why she called me and told me to stay away from her. *Okay... No need to address that.* Her boyfriend, on the other hand, might be the reason she chose to tell me to go away instead of run.

"You said, boyfriend. Do you live with your boyfriend?" I ask.

"Yes, Zach. Sorry I lied. I just wanted to protect him. He's a surgical resident at New York Pres-byterian."

"Does he know you're in hiding?"

"Yes, he does," she whispers. "But he's not coming home tonight. He has a long shift. I just tried calling him earlier but he's not answering. He'll be worried when he gets my message, though."

I catch Jasper looking at me through the rearview mirror again. I decide to avoid his eyes. This is what I do best, get information. He should just relax and let me work.

Kat confesses that Nel had no idea her daughter, Alexia, was still in touch with her. All of her life, Kat had been held prisoner in the small house in Chattanooga.

"Did you know your mother?" I ask.

Jasper readjusts in his seat. If he could tell me to keep quiet without alarming Kat, I know he would. He's oddly careful with her around. I think it's because he's programmed to take care of his family, and Kat, even though he barely knows her, is his family.

"I think so. I don't know..." She grows silent for a few beats. "I think Beth was my mom. She was older, but she hardly spoke to me or anyone else. For the longest time, I thought she was mute, but she was just so screwed up that she didn't like to talk—although, whenever slimy guys came to the house, she pointed forcefully at a crawl space under the floor, telling me to hide. I think she and I were the only two people who knew it existed."

She goes on to explain how the secret space led to the woods behind the house. "It was creepy serial-killer stuff."

Kat would crawl in the dirt with the spiders,

mice, and other insects and arrive at a five-by-five dusty space, where she would climb a set of fragile wooden steps to a hatch that opened in the woods.

I recall my visit to Chattanooga and remember the trees behind her old house. Kat says she would roam the woods, contemplating running away forever. However, she didn't know where to go. She had no education, no money, and—according to Bam, the man who ran the house—no common sense. He tried to convince her that she was nothing more than a stupid girl whose only value was what was between her legs.

"But I never believed a damn thing he said, especially that," she says.

Now that she's talking, it's difficult to get her to stop, which is a good thing as far as journalism is concerned. The wheel is turning and now all I have to do is listen as she provides answers to questions I haven't even asked. Jasper is super quiet too. He's listening and learning too. *You're welcome Jasper Blackstone.*

"It was snowing on the day I met Alexia," she says. "Beth had just gotten her teeth knocked out by a john, and she was in so much pain..." Kat took a deep breath through her nose. "Anyway, I was sitting against a tree, wearing nothing but a gown. It felt like my blood was frozen. All I wanted to do was die."

Then she explains how Alexia had found her in the woods and snuck her inside of Nel's house to warm her up and feed her.

"She asked me a lot of questions I couldn't answer, like what my name was, how old I was, and where my parents were. I couldn't even tell her where I lived because I was afraid she'd tell Bam that I'd snuck out of the house. But after my nightgown had dried, she gave me a coat and some shoes, and we promised to stay friends."

"How old were you?" I ask.

"I was fifteen."

"And you didn't know your name?"

She shook her head. "But I asked Beth if she knew, and she wrote something on a piece of paper, handed it to me, and whispered that I should never let anyone find it. Whenever she talked, she whispered." Kat says that last part as though it were an afterthought.

"Humph," I say. Bryn also whispers a lot. *Very interesting.* "What did Beth write?"

"She wrote my first name and age," she whispers, sounding exactly like Bryn.

Jasper caught that too because our eyes meet for

a moment. Thankfully, he stopped squirming in his seat and chastising me with his eyes through the rearview mirror. He's graciously letting me ask questions. I love that about him. Jasper is not an egomaniac who has to push his way or the highway. He has the ability to steer the ship and knows when to step back and let someone else take the wheel all the while remaining the commander.

I really want to fuck your brains out right now, I think as we catch eyes again in the mirror. But I'm also one hundred percent focused on getting as much out of Kat as I can during this car ride.

"Were the women and girls who lived in your house prostitutes?" I ask, remembering that Gina is or was a prostitute.

She drops her head as she nods.

It sounds like she wasn't a prostitute because the woman named Beth kept her safe. "Do you know what happened to Beth?"

Kat shakes her head.

"Do you remember what she looked like?"

"Sweetheart, that's enough questions," Jasper says.

Suddenly Kat flicks her attention onto Jasper as if it just occurred to her that we are romantically linked.

"So the two of you are a couple?" she asks.

Jasper glances at her in the passenger seat. Then he watches me through the rearview mirror. "Why don't you answer, babe?" he finally says, smirking sexily.

I snort a chuckle just as my phone rings. It's Rich.

"We're a thing," I admit. "I have to take this."

I'm smiling giddily at Jasper. For the moment, I'm going to forget how complicated it will be to walk off into the sunset with the man of my dreams. Also, a call from Rich, who's always the bearer of exciting news has me excited.

"Hey Rich," I say.

"Holly. You're not going to believe this."

Ooh... I'm already loving how this call is starting. I switch my device to the other ear. "I'm listening."

And then he tells me something that blows my mind.

WE ARRIVE at the airfield for a helicopter ride to a place Jasper calls Location Z. I've been quiet, tortured ever since learning some very ominous news about Amelia Blackstone. I'm not sure how Jasper is going to take what I have to tell him. After he collects Kat's suitcase and hands it off to a porter, I quickly step up beside him and say that I have to talk to him. Jasper nods sharply as if he already knows this.

Kat's eyes dance around in her sockets nervously now that she's been told we're not going with her. I watch impressed as Jasper tells her the porter's name and has her shake his hand and then he does the same with the pilot. He really puts her at ease when Jasper texts Zach, her boyfriend, his phone number, and business address. Jasper lets me know that he'll be right back. Kat and I wave goodbye to each other. I say that I'll see her later and then I watch them walk inside the terminal.

I pace along the vehicle as I wait. I'm nervous. What I have to tell Jasper is *the* story. It's the one best-selling biographies are made of. It's also the one that break hearts and causes public backlash. It's the story that I can't sit on. Due to the nature of the findings, Rich is only giving me forty-eight hours before he sends the results to the FBI.

I stop pacing to see Kat and Jasper in the distance. Kat stands with her shoulders curved, hugging herself while nodding. She appears so tiny next to those two big guys. Then Jasper commands my full attention. What a presence he has—so commanding, so sexy, and very safe. I focus on Kat again. She's timid, but I can tell she isn't afraid. She feels secure.

Finally, Jasper pats the pilot on the shoulder. He says something to the pilot who puts a reassuring hand on Jasper's shoulder. I've noticed over the years how much men touch each other. Women, we have the words, but men have the touch. And they need it —to be touched. I always wondered if it's because the lack of touch and tenderness males experience at the early age where boys are forced to "man-up." Or perhaps it's just something in their biology that makes them gravitate to touch as far as human connection more than words.

After one last nod, Jasper stands off as the pilot helps Kat into the aircraft. She waves at Jasper before fully entering and he waves back. Gosh, I love him. Just that one act makes me love him more, and I don't know why. He did nothing remarkable, all he did was wave goodbye to his long-lost half-sister.

My breaths grow deep and long as I watch Jasper walk back to me. I'm reeling the anticipation of being alone with him again. Soon, I'll have to tell him. How do I tell a man such news? I can't sit on this. I hope he understands that. But it's more than just work that has me all hot and ready. It's him. I confirmed to

Kat that he and I are indeed 'a thing'. Had I made a mistake?

He's in front of me now, standing so close that I can feel his exquisite energy wash over me.

"You suggested we remain behind. I'm guessing it has something to do with the conversation you had with Rich?" He says Rich's name like he reviles just a little.

Frowning so hard that I feel the tension in my forehead, I nod stiffly. "It does."

His eyes smolder as he uses two fingers to even out the lines in my forehead. Then, those two fingers journey down the side of my skin. "Umm," Jasper moans and then parts his lips.

I swallow hard.

"Then let's hear it." He clears his throat. "After..."

Jasper opens the door to the large back seat of the SUV.

WE'RE SEATED beside each other. He's looking into my eyes and I'm held captive by his. Suddenly, his face inches its way close to mine but I reluctantly press my palm against his chest, stopping before we kiss because if we kiss, there'll be no stopping us from going to second-base. My head is swimming in the energy that always swirls around us before sex ensues. There's no way I should delay saying this to him.

My eyes closed, and steadying my breaths, I whisper, "The DNA of your mother, Amelia Blackstone, matched that of a girl who was kidnapped thirty-five years ago. She was twelve years old then. Her name was Doris Hollander."

Jasper's eyes are no longer lidded. His expression is frozen in awe. *There's more. Is he ready to hear more?*

He covers his face with his large hands as he rests his head against the seat.

I keep waiting for him to say something, anything. Seconds tick by. It's torture giving him time to work out what I just dropped on him like a big fat bomb. I hate that in the end, after I reveal it all, I'm going to ask him for a favor.

"There's another thing," I say in a small voice.

It feels as if the molecules in the air are closing in on us as he finally removes his hands and looks at me. I tell him that Rich is giving me forty-eight hours before he submits the findings. The FBI is going to want to know who submitted the DNA for testing.

"For a reporter, that can get a little hairy, so I was wondering..."

"Done," he says without hesitation.

"Done?"

He takes my hand in his. "You want me to say that I submitted the DNA? Done."

I stare at his face. My heart, throat, and nostrils feel tight. It's true—Jasper Blackstone has become the one man in my entire life that I can count on. This feeling is brand-new, and I have no idea what to do with them. I don't want to cry. I don't want to show him how lacking I am. Jasper takes care of everybody—his sisters, brothers, father, and employees, just everybody. *Am I special to him?* I have never been special to anybody.

He kisses the back of my hand. "You were right to tell me this before we boarded the helicopter."

I swallow so that I won't sound choked up. "I thought it was the right thing to do." *Good, that came out clearly.*

He takes my hand and interlaces our fingers. "I have a contact with the FBI."

I snort a chuckle. "I'm not surprised."

"But in forty-eight hours it's going to be a shit-show."

I nod, agreeing. "I've learned the best way to

avoid a shit-show is to control the narrative." I sigh defeated. "But we need information that we just don't have to do that."

Jasper grunts and then abruptly adjusts to sit on the edge of his seat to look out the front window. "We should get going."

I join him by scooting to the edge of my seat. "To... What did you call it, Location Z?"

"To my place in the city," he says.

I look at him incredulously. "Oh."

"Yes."

Valentine's warning for me to stay away from Jasper comes howling back into my memory. "Do you think that's a good idea?"

He stares at me for a moment and then caresses the side of my face. "Don't be afraid, babe. I said I'm handling Valentine, and I am. There's nothing he can do to you if you're with me."

I agree. But still, returning to the city together seems like a big gamble. "What about Julia? Where's she?"

"Stay put," Jasper says, then opens his door. He puts one foot on the cement and then says, "And Julia's exactly where she's supposed to be."

FOUR

DEFINITELY, US...

HOLLY HENDERSON

We take to the skies and ride back to the city in a helicopter. Jasper's on the phone with his FBI contact, letting him or her know that the evidence will be submitted but to hold it until he gives the okay to release it to investigators.

"Yes, forty-eight hours, that's all," he says.

I can't look away from Jasper. Each time I try to deny it, I can't: Like a fully blossomed rose of spring, I am in love with Jasper Blackstone. Even if our relationship ends badly, I'm content with knowing that the love we've made, the conversations we've had, and just being near him are the best things I've ever experienced.

He's doing more listening than talking. He's also staring at me without focus. Mostly he says, "yes" and "that's right." Finally, he says, "I know" as if he's irritated. It's clear he gets what he wants when he says, "Thank you—thank you very much." He ends the call.

I smile at him and he winks his eyebrows twice. That look in his eyes tells me he wants to pick up where we left off before I broke the news about Amelia. I want the same thing. We don't break eye contact until the helicopter hovers over a helipad on the top of a towering building. *So this is where Jasper lives.* His residence isn't that far from BCN studios. Once the aircraft touches down an attendant, who is muscular, opens the door for us. Jasper exits first and then holds my hand as I step out into the freezing temperatures. To beat the cold, he curls an arm around me and together we race toward a lit hallway where two more burly men stand at each side of the entrance.

The change in temperature from outside to the inside is jarring. Jasper's hand is strong and warm, and that's enough to keep my body temperature perfectly regulated. However, if this hallway is an indication of how the rest of Jasper's place looks, then we're off to a stunning start. The pristine white walls have gorgeous black and white photos of New York City hung on them. I'm amazed how quiet it is as we walk on plush black carpet. Not even a decibel of the helicopter's rumbling engine can be heard. The fact that Jasper's security was pretty tight isn't lost on me either.

We reach a steel-plated elevator.

"How did you like the ride?" he asks as he uses his thumbprint to open the elevator doors.

My eyes feel brighter and my smile sexier. "It was lovely."

His eyebrows raise as Jasper makes room for me to enter first.

"Thank you," I say.

Our formalities is merely a flirtation ritual.

Then, he's inside with me. Jasper's arms are around me and my back is against the mirror-glass wall.

"Finally, I have you all to myself." His words come out hot and heavy on my lips.

We kiss—feverishly, greedily, as if we have only one more time to do this and then never again. The elevator ride is short, only one floor up. The doors slide open. Jasper ends our kiss, leaving me light-headed as gray light from the dank day filling the space catches my attention. I want so much right now. I want to take our making out to the next level, but I also want to see the kind of place that Jasper keeps. I want to see what his space looks like when it belongs fully to him.

As if hypnotized, I walk out of the elevator and look around.

"Wow," I say, taking it all in.

This is nothing like the Blackstone mansion. The place is very modern, and everything inside it—including the floor to high-ceiling windows showcasing the New York skyline—stands out. The furniture is a collection of comfy black-leather sofas and chairs with silver armrests and legs. A large black, white, and silver coffee table is the central point for all the furniture. There are matching long silver tables with decorative pieces made of metal, crystal, ivory, and obsidian. The furniture sits on a humongous area rug that has a design of a black-and-white photo of the back of a young woman in a sundress, her hair blowing in the wind as she stands at the edge of the shoreline, looking toward a lighthouse on top of a rock cliff. I can't look away from the graphic. I feel as if I've seen the landscape before.

"Was that shot taken at the Blackstone mansion?" I ask, pointing at the rug.

When I turn, Jasper's attention laps me up like he's already indulging in me.

"Yes," he replies in a silken voice.

I'm torn between closing the distance between us and letting him have me sooner rather than later, and continuing my exploration. I must see more. And since he is giving me the freedom to take it all in, I fold my arms over my chest and continue my tour. There are lots of black-and-white landscapes on the wall. I stop in front of a still photo with the younger versions of Jasper, Spencer, and Asher, their shirtless arms around each other's necks, smiling as if they are the epitome of happiness and brotherhood. They are boys, really, on their way to becoming men. Their smiles make me smile. There's another photo of Bryn with a hand covering one side of her face as she plays coy for the camera. I've never seen her that way before—happy, youthful, innocent. She has to be about fifteen or sixteen years old.

"Who took these?" I ask, standing in front of the photo of Bryn.

Jasper is now standing beside me. "Amelia did."

I gasp softly. "Wow."

I watch Jasper study the rest of the photos, but this time, I look at them differently, as though I'm looking through the window to Amelia Blackstone's soul while remembering she more than likely had been kidnapped. But by who? Certainly not Randolph Blackstone.

Jasper and I move to a photo of two little boys in sailor suits, running on the grass and holding up toy airplanes, the bay in the distance. Then we go to one of a teenage version of Jasper standing at the window but turning to look over his shoulder while smiling at the camera. He looks so burdened.

"How old are you here?" I ask.

After a few moments of study, he shakes his head. "I don't know." He's sounds surprised by his omission.

I can't take my eyes off his profile. Watching him makes my heart swell like a balloon. And it's more than seeing him so vulnerable, it's the family photos. They're making me remember feelings long forgotten.

I loop my arm around his waist. "I wish I would've known you at that age. I bet you wouldn't have even given me a second look." I laugh softly. "Actually, I take that back, I bet you would've thought I was a scrawny, lanky thing, whose school uniforms were always two sizes too big. My dad..." Something my dad used to say drops in my head like a repressed memory gliding to the surface.

I swallow to loosen my tight voice as tears burn the backs of my eyes. "He used to say that his daughter would only attend schools where the kids wear uniforms. He thought that kids who were going to be important one day would only go to those schools." The corners of my lips pull down into a somber smile. "I just remembered that."

When I turn to Jasper, he kisses my forehead. "I wish the same."

My eyes are closed as he continues pelting my forehead with gentle kisses. "But you looked too serious to be interested in a girl like me."

"I was serious," he says as he starts trailing kisses down the side of my face. "But then there would be the smell of you, the way you look at me, and how you make me feel when you're near, and all of my defenses would've been obliterated."

I tilt my head back and naturally his lips meet mine. We engage in a soft, sensuous kiss. I'm certain this is what he means by the smell of me, the nearness of me and the way I make him feel. All of those components of Jasper draw me to him like the pull of a magnet. But then there's this—the taste of his silken tongue coiling around mine.

Jasper expels a long breath as his lips disengage with mine. His erection presses against my belly. I know what he wants. I want it too. But he closes his eyes, takes another breath, and then says, "I brought you to this room for a reason."

My eyes are closed and my desire is aflame. "You did?"

"Yes," he sighs.

Gradually, he takes in the photos again, and even though I want his hands all over and him inside me, I'm also curious to hear more. I've learned this important lesson—if Jasper is speaking, then he's saying something worth listening too. It's one of the many mounting reasons why I've come to the point where I don't think I could ever live without him.

"I didn't know this film existed until after my mother died. I used to see her with her camera every now and then, snapping photos here and there, but she never had the film developed."

We let silence linger as Jasper collects his thoughts.

"She didn't take one photo where my brothers and sister and I weren't happy. But we were unhappy most of the time," he says.

"You must've loved her an awful lot."

He nods gently. "I did. I do."

Then I'm struck by a very heartbreaking thought. "How are you dealing with the possibility that your mother may have been abducted?"

"I want my mother's soul to rest in peace. That's how I feel about it."

"I understand," I whisper, I truly do.

He takes me by the hand and draws me to him. Even through his thick coat I can feel his hard body. "I want to make love to you again, but we both know it wouldn't be the best use of our time right now."

I grin. *Truly, that is such a Jasperish thing to say.* "No, it wouldn't."

"Then can I ask you some questions?" I raise an eyebrow inquisitively. "Some journalistic questions?"

He exhales briskly as he rolls his eyes just a little. "Like what?"

I take his response as a passport to ask away. "Well, everyone knows you are the powerhouse behind BFE and were even before your father died. You could've destroyed Randolph with your pinkie finger if you wanted. So have you wondered why your mother never told you she'd been kidnapped?"

"My guess is that she didn't want to leave me with him. She couldn't leave and take me with her. He would've hunted her down, killed her family and then stolen us back. That's how Randolph operated."

"Wow." I'm nearly breathless.

"Amelia was smart," he continues. "She knew my father was a sociopath, but she taught me to not fear him. She would say that he was a predator but I was a hunter and the predator knows the hunter is superior." Suddenly, his frown intensifies. I'm acquainted with that look on his face.

"What is it?" I ask.

"I just had a memory, I think."

I nod encouragingly.

His face grows dark. "I was asleep—at least, my mother thought I was. She would often use the secret passageways to enter my room and check on me. Once, after I had a bad couple of days with my father's special kind of grooming, which involved torture"—he snarls as he sniffs like an angry animal—"I couldn't move my arms or legs, and I ached all over, and in the dark, she sat by my bed and said, 'We're still here because you're going to make him pay, son. You're going to take everything he has and leave him with filth.'" Jasper takes me by the hand. "I want to show you something."

HE DOESN'T LET GO of my hand as he leads me up a curved set of stairs. When we make it to the top, he steals a quick kiss from me. We both tremble with delight from how divine that short but delicious kiss felt and tasted. We continue the journey through Jasper's stunning apartment high in the sky. We pass through a great foyer on the next floor. I think this is the main level. We walk through an atrium which has north and south views of the city. We pass another small living space. The furniture is bright red and velvet. Journeying further down the hallway, a light aroma of food cooking makes my stomach growl.

"You're hungry?" Jasper asks.

I'm shocked he heard that. "Um, yeah."

"We'll eat soon. However, Bart isn't here today. He's at the other location. I thought we'd be there tonight, but things have changed, of course."

"You do know that I'm not averse to cooking for the both of us. As a matter of fact, I can make a mean meal as long as I have a solid recipe," I say.

His lopsided grin is so sexy. "I'm sure you can cook, babe, but you'll enjoy Deb's food just as much as Art's." His lust-filled eyes pass over my face. "Plus, you won't have time to cook when this is over."

My eyebrows raise in surprise. "When this is over? Where are you taking me?"

"To my office," he says, leading me in a different direction from the delicious scent.

We pass a bedroom and then another one and we enter his magnificent office. I mean, if I had an office like this, I would've never rented a space downtown.

The width of his desk competes with the span of the large windows, and his big chair sits in the middle. Tall cabinets stand on each side of the wall. A wide-screen television, which folds out from a bracket attached to the ceiling, is in the center of the room. A conference table is on one side of the room with eight white leather rolling chairs around it. There's something very sexy about the set up.

Jasper walks over to open a cabinet drawer as I continue being awed about the sheer size and scope of the space. It costs a lot of money to live this large in New York City. I often forget how much of it Jasper has. Personally, having a lot of money has never been my goal. But then what has been my goal? Maybe this—maybe it's love. True, unconditional, unbreakable love. But is that what this is?

"Holly," Jasper calls, which I now realize is for the second time.

I quickly turn to face him. "Yes."

"Are you okay?"

I put on a smile. "I'm fine."

Jasper's eyes narrow and then open back up. He's holding up a tin box. "Here it is."

I grunt, intrigued. "What's that?"

"It's a box of Amelia's things." Jasper points at the conference table. "Let's go sit."

Jasper pulls out a chair for me to sit in and then sits beside me. My nerves are on edge as he opens the tin box, which has red, pink, blue, and white paisleys on it.

"Whoa," I say once the lid is off. "When was the last time you opened this?"

He glances at me, and holds the box as if what's inside is very precious to him. " Two days after my mother died."

My eyes are wide taking in all the items. "There is so much here to unpack."

"When you mentioned controlling the narrative, we can do that. And this will help us."

Jasper is not that much older than I am. What's so funny is that when I first met him, he reminded me of a man pushing forty. But right now, his youthful manliness is pure perfection, so handsome and so sexy. He's transformed since I first met him.

"Us?" I ask, beaming.

He smirks. "Definitely, us."

FIVE

DISCOVERY

HOLLY HENDERSON

Inside the box, and among other keepsakes, is a Princess Leia action figure and a piece of denim with the name Doris embroidered on it in yellow yarn.

Jasper seems vexed by his thoughts. "She said Doris was a childhood friend."

I rub his back consolingly. "You couldn't have known she wasn't telling the truth."

His brisk exhale, the way he's shaking his leg impatiently, I can tell my words went in one ear and out the other. "But deep down, I could tell something was wrong." Jasper groans as he wipes his hands up and down his face. Then, on another brisk exhale he says, "I turned a blind eye to Randolph's..." He exhales. "He had a demon inside of him. I could see it looking at me through his eyes, daring me."

I'm chilled to the bone. I've seen that sort of evil that he's talking about. "How do you think he got that way?"

"Abuse."

"What kind of abuse?"

Jasper gazes into my eyes. I would think he'd look burdened because of his current emotional state but he doesn't. His skin glows and his sad eyes gleam. It's as if purging himself of these revelations has somehow lightened his load. But I can also sense the wall that just shot up between us. Jasper is not going to answer my question. I didn't expect him to. Not yet at least.

"Too soon," I say, rubbing his thigh.

He looks down at my hand. It's not like he's troubled by my touch but I steal a cursory glance at his crotch. It's ballooning. *Oh...* I remove my hand. "Yes. Too soon. But..."

Jasper takes a key out of a box and holds it up. "My mother lived for one thing, and one thing only."

I know what that is. "Payback?"

"Yes, retribution."

I nod at the key between his large fingers. "Do you think that opens something at the Blackstone mansion?"

"I think so," he whispers, sounding absorbed by his thoughts.

My cellphone rings in my purse. "Sorry," I say as I take it out and look to see who's calling. "Shit. It's Kylie. I'm supposed to give her an update on what I found."

Jasper's doing that thing where he rubs the side of his face. "How well do you know her professionally?" he asks.

I silence the phone. That look on his face worries me.

"I know her well." I feel as if he just asked me a trick question. "Listen, Jasper. I know there's a lot of tension between the two of you. I mean, you've legally stopped her from investigating your family."

"Yes, because she went too far, Holly."

I shrug nonchalantly. "Yes, she was caught paying off a coroner. If she were able to get her hands on that information, it would've been factual and valuable."

If looks could kill, I'd be six feet under. "That is not the point, Holly." He enunciates every syllable.

My goodness, he is pissed.

I don't feel like letting him off the hook. If he's going to sully Kylie's reputation, whatever he has on her had better stink to high heaven.

"I believe in a strong and free press, but Kylie is a dangerous journalist who will do whatever the hell it takes to obtain the desired results."

I throw my hands up. "Prove it."

First, Jasper tilts his head, assessing me as if he's processing the fact that I just issued him a dare. Then, he holds his head upright, nods once vigorously then rises to his feet. I'm experiencing that floating feeling as I watch him walk to the file cabinet and press a number on a keypad to unlock it. I had forgotten—Jasper doesn't make unproven accusation. I'm almost afraid of what he has on Kylie.

When Jasper returns to the table, he calmly sets a thick folder in front of me and opens it. "Go ahead. Read it."

WE'VE VEERED off subject just so that Jasper can prove that my friend cannot be trusted. After my stomach growled yet again, and Jasper asked his kitchen staff to bring us a late lunch of peppercorn-encrusted prime rib with roasted carrots, and butter and herb risotto. He stepped out to handle some business in private. I'm reading one page at a time while eating. The pages are all proof that Kylie has an issue with the truth. Jasper has acquired twenty-three articles that Kylie had written where she presented names of people who don't exist to editors, claiming them to be deep background sources. But the clincher is the fact that she had been in contact with another journalist who was working on the same story. I am reading indisputable evidence that Kylie has been shadow writing stories along with other journalists but submitting her articles to editors by confirming her fake sources before the other journalists could confirm his or her real sources.

Jasper comes back into the room just as one story in particular catches my eye. I tap the pages. "Wait. This is mine."

He closes the distance between us. "The story about the minor leagues scandal?" He sits in the chair beside me again.

"Yeah," I'm only barely able to say. I feel so betrayed by her.

I spent weeks working on, uncovering a criminal element who made a lot of money fixing minor-league-championship games.

"Unbelievable," I say while reading the proof. "She called me after her article was published to apologize for not letting me know she was working on the same story. Of course, I asked her how she knew I was investigating the group. She said one of her sources told her they spoke to me. I thought it was strange, but I believed her because I had no reason to doubt her." I cock my head as I remember something else. "But the entire article was eventually retracted because..."

"Three sources said she lied." Jasper read the names off another page. "But those people didn't exist. The paper merely covered their asses. Read this." He hands me what appears to be a short report on the revoked story. A guy named Peter Fordham, who was one of the sources that I'd actually interviewed, emailed Dennis Thompson, the editor who used to publish all of Kylie's bunk articles, to say that he could confirm that her sources didn't exist and the information being claimed by them was fraudulent. Instead of challenging Peter, Dennis chose to pull the article.

"So Dennis knows," I whisper. He's the editor in chief of *Journalistic Weekly Report,* also known as *JWR.* "No wonder I could never get anything published in *JWR.*"

I close the folder and squeeze my lips together, angrier than a bull seeing red. I don't need to read anymore. "Does she know about this?"

Jasper nods once.

My jaw drops. "Is this the leverage you have on her?"

"Yes."

"Why haven't you told me before now?"

"I am bound by our agreement, Holly. She's dangerous. Even a hint of her false reporting could ruin my family."

I jerk my head back with a grunt. I'm hardly able to believe what I'm hearing. "Does everything come down to you protecting your family?"

"Yes, Holly," he says sternly. "Protecting my family always comes first."

We engage in a stare down of epic proportions. My jaw is clenched, and I can't stop shaking my head. I want to run away from him as fast as I can. I tell myself, *See? This is why he can't be trusted. He will do whatever it takes to save his family's reputation.* Yet... Here we sit, digging into an old box that belonged to his mother. Also, it's not like he's using his influence to shut down Rich's findings regarding his mother. I'm sure he could if he truly wanted to.

Finally, he sits back in his chair, taking the tension out of his body. The tip of his finger lands hard on the folder full of Kylie's lies. "I'm breaking my agreement with Kylie Neeland by showing you this."

I nod stiffly, acquiescing. "I know."

"Believe me, I never planned on letting her get away with this for long. Every crook meets their demise and she will meet hers."

I look down at my cell phone on the table, contemplating all that I've discovered. Then I'm struck by a new thought which sends anger coursing through me. "She wants to destroy you, Jasper. And she wants me to do it for her. But the irony is she knows how I feel about you which means she's being particularly cruel, to you and to me." I'm even angrier. "How could I have been so stupid?"

Jasper takes my hand in his. "You're not stupid. You're the smartest person I know."

My heart is beating so fast that I can hardly breathe. Tears burn the back of my eyes. However, after Jasper said I'm the smartest person he knows, I don't feel so stupid anymore. I want revenge, though. I want to stop Kylie in her tracks.

"I know what I have to do," I say, grinning impishly.

Jasper raises a brow inquisitively.

"I'll feed her fake details about Eve slash Kat complete with fake sources, giving her exactly what she needs to beat me to the story." I wink at him.

Jasper smirks. "You have a dark side, I see."

"I wouldn't call it that. I'd call it..." I twist my mouth, searching for the right words. "Being an agent of proper retribution."

I've seen a snake strike its prey, darting forward so fast that it catches the rodent off guard. That's how quick Jasper guides me to my feet and draws me against him. His delicious tongue explores the depths of my mouth. Hands on my waist, Jasper hoists me off my feet. I wrap my legs around his torso as he carries me. My face feels so delicate held between his large hands. I sigh softly, experiencing a balmy sensation rise through me as he plants gentle but fervent kisses at the side of my mouth and up my cheek. He moans as I return the favor and kiss his smoothly shaven face. Then, my butt comes down on top of his oversized office desk.

I'm shivering from want as we hold and deepen our eye contact. Jasper takes off my right shoe and tosses it over his shoulder then he does the same to my left shoe. He slowly runs a hand up my heated crotch, stopping at my clit to rub.

I suck air as sensations swirl through my sex.

Jasper's left eyebrow flits up. "You like that?"

Releasing a long breath through my nose, I nod jerkily. Then he frees me from my black panties.

"How does the desk feel?" his whisper is infused with lust.

I twist my hips to get comfortable, and he must see traces of agony on my face, because he picks me up and sets me in his big comfortable leather chair. His lidded eyes drink me in. I arch my back, battling the urge to squirm with need.

"Spread your legs," he commands.

Hands squeezing the armrests, I do as I'm told.

Jasper inhales deeply. His chest rises high as his lungs expand. Then he forces the air out as he falls to his knees. A moan escapes me as he takes me by the thighs, possessing them. He tugs my ass toward his mouth. His eyes are still on me as I feel the soft, warm, delicate but ravenous stimulation of his tongue, breath, and pressure against my clit.

The gratification is immediate. I squeeze the arms of the chair, but that brings me no relief from his pleasurable assault.

"Oh, ah, oh..." I suck air through my teeth. I feel each stroke of his tongue on every part of my clit—the top, the bottom, the right, the left, and every place between.

My cries become louder and louder and louder. I try to move my hips away from his stimulation, but he has me fastened in place.

"Jasper, oh, Jasper, please." He's watching his handiwork as our eyes connect.

"Oh..." My head presses against the seat.

The sensation abruptly changes as stimulation moves from one side of my clit to the other. A new orgasm is building and building, and then...explosion. I cry out to the Almighty. It seems as if the orgasm will never end. My sex pulsates. Jasper slides his fingers inside me so he can feel it.

"Mm," he moans like he loves to feel my sex jump with orgasm.

"It feels so..." I suck air as if I'm drowning in the sea of sensations. My hands are still searching for a solid place to land until my fingers grip his scalp.

"Umm..." he moans, seeming to like how I'm touching him.

And then I come again. And he still doesn't stop. His tongue has moved to the top of my clit, his fingers are still inside me, rubbing. *My goodness.* I have never felt such a thing in my life. It feels as though my orgasm is building in several spots. *How can this be?*

"Jasper, baby," I say with a whimper.

"Mm..." he moans without stopping.

"Oh, baby," I cry.

His grunt reverberates.

"Oh, baby!" *What the...* My mouth remained caught open, and I struggle to breathe.

The blast of orgasm saturates every single area of my sex. As pleasure stretches like vines, I white out. Someone is screaming Jasper's name, and it takes a moment to realize that someone is me. Suddenly, I'm lifted out of my chair and set on top of Jasper's desk. I know what he wants, but when I reach out to undo his pants, he's beat me to the punch. His cock is out and so hard that it's pointing high.

Jasper breathes heavily through his nose, his teeth clenched, with one hand, he grabs his cock to guide it into my wetness, and with the other, he gripped my ass to crush me against his erection. When the two meet, he soars inside me so deep that I feel him in my belly. Jasper's lust for me has risen past a tolerable level.

His cock moves in and out of me.

"Oh," he repeats, mouth caught open like he's already on the verge of blowing.

"Yes, baby," I sigh.

We kept our hazy gazes on each other's face. "I love you," I mouth.

Then, with one hard plunge into my slippery heat, he quivers and belts my name.

JASPER and I hold each other for a while after he comes.

"Baby, we're flying out to Newport tonight," he finally whispers thickly.

"Okay," I whisper too. I want more of him. So much more of him. "But why?"

"I have an idea about what the key in my mother's box might open."

SIX

NARRATIVES

HOLLY HENDERSON

The office holds the unique scent that arises whenever Jasper and I make love. It's sweet and spicy and divinely sensual. I can't put my panties back on—they are way too wet for that. Jasper calls his housekeeper and directs her to bring us two white fluffy robes and slippers. After we strip out of the rest of our clothes, including our underwear, she takes our garments to wash and press and have them back to us before Jasper and I leave. We'll be leaving after midnight. Due to the weather conditions, we're riding in his private airplane and not the helicopter. That gives us five hours before heading to Teterboro.

The atmosphere is peaceful and cozy. The only other person I ever felt this comfortable lounging around is Bryn, Jasper's sister. It's like he and I fit together like two puzzle pieces. I watch Jasper pad over to the file cabinet to put away the folder he has on Kylie as I sit in his executive chair. I eye him curiously as he presses numbers on the keypad.

"I thought you moved to LA," I say.

The keypad beeps, indicating the lock has been engaged. "I was living in LA full-time."

"But now?"

"I'm here."

"Why?"

He freezes and then looks at me. There is no lack of trust forming his expression, only a sexy and amused half smile. "You for one."

I stroke my lips wanting so desperately to kiss his. "And for two?"

"BCN and BFE."

"Ahh... I almost forgot, the hostile takeover," I say as if I'm making a dramatic announcement.

Jasper laughs, a real, pure, genuine laugh. I absolutely love the sound of it.

"And by the way, the purchase of BCN is nearly a done deal." His lips twitch up into a victorious grin. "Katherine had attempted to outbid us but her biggest investor couldn't come up with the funds."

"Was that investor Valentine?" I laugh.

"Damn it, you're so damn smart. It turns me on."

"Oh," I say not at all feigning my surprise. "That was actually a guess."

He tilts his head curiously. "Really?"

I nod vigorously. "Really."

His eyebrows bounce twice. "You're still brilliant baby."

I'm simpering, which I never done a lot of before meeting Jasper. He makes me simper. "By the way, I'm still not interested in working in television, even if you are the big boss."

He grunts thoughtfully as he finishes putting away the file.

Now that sounded like he's holding a ton of mysteries in his head. "So, really, you didn't buy BCN because I took a job there?" I ask to flush out his thoughts.

Jasper closes the file cabinet and then leans against it in a casual, relaxed way. "As I said before, I didn't submit my bid to purchase BCN to control you, Holly. A good friend of mine, Vincent Adams, came to me with an offer a while back. I looked at the specs and thought it would be a good investment."

"Oh," I say, surprised. "Vincent Adams of AEE?"

"Yes."

"Wow, great business partner."

He nods in agreement as a veil of distress falls over his face.

"What are you thinking?" I ask.

"I'm thinking, if we don't get ahead of this story, I might not appear to be the best candidate to purchase a news organization."

"Right," I say, suddenly struck by that illumination. "Right..."

"Listen," he says and then walks towards me. "We don't have much time before we get out of here, so..." He's standing in front of me, hands outstretched, waiting. I put my hands on top of his and he grabs hold and guides me to my feet.

We gaze into each other's eyes. There's no doubt about it, the mood has just shifted.

Jasper tilts his head toward the hallway. His eyes are telling me he's ready to get out of here.

With a smile as faint but pure as the Mona Lisa's, I nod.

———

AS JASPER HOLDS MY HAND, my head spins as we tread down a long hallway. We cross the threshold of a stylish yet comfortable bedroom. Jasper peels my robe off, and I take his off. Skin on skin, we fall onto his king-sized bed and roll around on it, kissing in our sensual way, our tongues gliding, teeth nibbling, and fingers stimulating each other's erogenous zones.

I love licking and gently raking my teeth against Jasper's nipples. I love how his powerful body quickens beneath me until he can't stand it any longer. Then he takes me and flips me onto my back. My mind and body feel as if they are floating before both hit the mattress. He does the same thing to me that I did to him.

"Hey, babe," I say after moaning from the sensual feeling of his warm mouth stimulating my nipples.

He raises his chest to look at me with lidded eyes. "Hmm?"

"What was that you did earlier in your office? When you went down on me. It was like... I never knew that could happen to my body."

"Then you liked it?" he asks, grinning proudly.

"Very much so."

His eyes shift like he's processing his thoughts. "I'd never done that before, actually. But I've gotten a feel for your body. I know where to touch you, where to stimulate you to make you climax."

"Really?" I ask in a highly inquisitive tone. "I

mean that much to you that you'll learn my body?" I'm shamelessly fishing, but I don't care. I'll never get tired of hearing how much Jasper cares about me.

He smiles as his finger traces my eyebrows and skims the side of my face. "I know a lot about what you like."

"You do?"

Jasper's eyes burn with lust. "You always like it when I say this."

"Say what?"

He raises his eyebrows. "Spread your legs."

I'm caught in a state of euphoria. "Are you telling me?"

"I'm telling you to spread your legs."

I separate my thighs some more. Jasper's fingers delicately, methodically slipping in and out of me.

"Like this," he sighs, his breaths heavy with lust.

The immediacy of the spark of orgasm that I feel makes my eyes expand as the back of my head crashes into the pillow. Jasper doesn't stop. He keeps doing whatever the hell he's doing.

"If I increase my speed..."

I gasp. "I'm coming," I say in a ragged and breathy voice. I'm about to blow.

"If I slow it down..."

The orgasmic sensation subsides, but my hips chase his fingers to get it back.

"Ah, I see you want it." He's doing it fast again, and all that pleasure returns with a vengeance. "How hard do you want to come?"

I try to answer, "Hard." But all I can do is suck air, squeeze the ultra soft bed linens and enjoy the fantastic feeling.

"Say something, baby, or else..." He stops, and I lose the sensation again.

"Hard," I whisper thrashing my head from side to side, wanting him to finish me now.

His fingers are back inside me, rubbing that spot. It's brash of him to show me just how easily he can find it again and how quickly he can bring my body magnificent pleasure. Also, there is something about the way my body responds to him that puts that lustful haze in his eyes.

Jasper bends down to consume my hard nipples as he continues stimulating me.

I taste my bottom lip. Seriously... I'm about to pass out from experiencing sensory overload.

"How hard do you want to come?" he asks again, then bites my right nipple before pressing his soft, warm tongue over the ache.

"Hard," I strain to say.

And just like that, my wish is his command. Jasper's fingers work fast and faster. The sparks of orgasm gather and, moment by moment, intensifies until...

"Ah...Oh..." I cry out, my body quaking.

Once his fingers are out of me, I writhe with pleasure until all the sensations had subsided. "Oh my goodness, Jasper," I breathe heavily. "You *have* learned my body."

"More than you'll ever know."

When I turned to face him, I see that his cock is standing at attention.

"How about I do something for you." I reach out to wrap my hand around his cock.

He catches my hand before I reach his manhood and enfolds my fingers with his. "Not yet, babe. I have meetings before we head out. But enjoy a bath, watch some TV, order some dessert, rest. Whatever you want, my staff will get it for you. I want you completely comfortable here." He grabs hold of his cock. "And don't worry about this. I'm going to give you more than you can handle as soon as I'm done."

My gaze turns hazier as my eyes fall on his perfectly molded cock. "Later, then."

He kisses the back and then the palm of my hand. *I love it when he does that too.*

"You better believe it." Jasper springs to his feet with the energy of a gazelle. "And, babe, you're in hiding. Remember that."

I groan. "So that means you can work, but I can't?"

He hovers over me, pushing both hands onto the mattress. Our faces are so close that I have to lean back, or I'll be forced to kiss him.

"Do you have a problem with resting? Is that hard for you?" That sounds like a challenge.

"I can rest," I purr, although I haven't even convinced myself of that.

Jasper kisses me swiftly on the lips. "Good." He stands tall and assured.

I reach out to him as if trying to catch him before he gets away. "By the way, I wanted to ask you about Bryn. Have you heard any updates regarding her whereabouts?"

He veers away from me, that stony expression back on his face. "She's fine," he says as if it hurts him to reveal that.

My jaw drops. "Then you know where she is?"

"Yes. That's all I'm saying for now. Are you satisfied with that answer?"

His efficient tone, combined with his serious expression and nakedness, turns me on. Jasper must see the desire in my eyes and understands that the look on my face is the answer to his question. He cracks an impish smile.

"Thank you," he says. "I'd better go before you convince me to finish what I started."

I roll onto my belly, chuckling as I watch him trot into his walk-in closet. I'm so happy—one hundred percent filled with bliss. I never believed this could be me. Deep down, I don't trust it, but for the moment, I decide to go with it.

WHEN JASPER WALKS out of the closet, he's wearing a pair of nicely tailored navy-blue trousers with a light-blue button-down shirt. The sleeves are folded above his elbows, and the buttons are loose at his chest. He looks so sexy I can hardly stand it. On his way out, he kisses me again and reminds me that I am his. My mind is floating, and even though I didn't say it, I could hardly believe that he belongs to me.

Now that I'm alone, I think about how Jasper had asked if I have a problem with sitting still and relaxing. His bed is so comfortable. The blanket smells like him. I gather a bunch of the comforter, bring it to my nose and sniff. Umm... It's him. I roll onto my back and gaze unfocused at the ceiling.

Oddly, I'm not feeling anxious about getting up and going out to break my next big story. Although my next big story is in this incredible New York apartment with me. And he just made me come so hard that my body is still reeling from his stimulation. I pull up and lay on my side as my sex streaks with traces of that hard orgasm I experienced not too long ago.

Now that I think about it, the most rest I've ever gotten was during the first week and a half of the new year, when my heart was so broken I couldn't even get out of bed. I smash my eyes closed and wipe away the memory of lying in bed in my flannel pajamas, lamenting the loss of Jasper Blackstone. My eyes pop open. Good energy races through my body, and I'm ready to do exactly what Jasper has suggested.

First, I step into his locker-room-sized shower and use the shampoo that sits on a ledge in the corner. The warm water feels divine. When I'm done showering, I really overindulge in relaxation and take a bath. As I sit in the silky water, I fight the urge to think of my next work task. I was eager to figure out how we could possibly put out a story about Randolph Blackstone kidnapping his wife when she was a minor and then getting her pregnant. What he did was dark and sick. It's unbelievable actually. There's no way to spin the truth. Jasper definitely has to be the one to hold the press conference. He has to say that he has discovered the most disturbing details about his mother's life. That's it! He has to distance himself from Randolph, and associate himself with Amelia.

"Hmm..." I wonder if Jasper has already told Bryn about Amelia.

He clearly knows where she is, and is in touch with her.

And then there's Kylie and her fake sources. *How could she have done that?* I can still hardly believe it, but I can't deny what I saw with my own two eyes. I wonder what she has to say for herself. The longer I sat in the tub, the more I realize without a shadow of doubt that she was trying to play me. The pieces are right in front of my face, ready to be put together. Sure, I'm the one who called her while I stayed at the Blackstone mansion. I knew she had a fascination with the family, and I wanted to see if she could help me with the investigation that Bryn had paid me to do. So as far as good luck goes, I was the four-leaf clover that had fallen into her lap. I always thought the agreement between her and Jasper was strange. As I told Jasper, paying off a coroner wouldn't have destroyed her career. I squeeze my eyes shut and rub the inside corners as I wait for the disappointment to pass. Yes, Kylie has broken my heart. I thought we were friends. I know we are friends. I want her to prove to me that we are. And I know exactly what to do.

I rise to my feet and rich bubbles slide down my skin. Before stepping out of the tub, I stop to ponder. I can't make it hurt so badly that my actions will ruin Kylie forever. *But is there any other way to do it?*

But there was no other course of action. She's taken a new job as a TV host. A TV host is not a reporter. Journalists did the legwork—we comb through records, contact sources, ask for documents, and attempt to catch our subjects with their hands in the cookie jar, and those are only a fraction of all we do to get the story. Perhaps Kylie has finally arrived and is done pretending to be a real reporter.

I sit back down in the tub, deciding to let things be.

Although...

She stole my gambling story, and then let it die after her deception was discovered. Should I see that as water under the bridge? I recall our conversation in my suite, after Valentine and his goon accosted me. She only stopped by my room for one reason and one reason only. She wanted to know more details about Chattanooga. I stand back up. She needs to learn a lesson, and I will be the one to give it to her.

I DRY my skin and blow dry my hair. Now I sit on the edge of the bed, constructing a long email in Notes. I make up a story about how a source named Rosie has given me another address in Chattanooga, a place where a full-on brothel is being operated. I make up a name for the madam and validate her credentials, saying that this woman, who I call Leanne Dean, has gone on record stating that Randolph Blackstone was her premiere client. I add that Leanne can't confirm or deny the fact that other members of the Blackstone clan visited the brothel. I'm not sure whether or not it's a good idea to add that detail, but I know it will be fresh meat for her to maul to the bone. I make up names of prostitutes. I give her fake dates of the Blackstone men visits. Lastly, I tell her she can't reach me because I'm in hiding from Valentine but an editor, who I call D, is expecting the story before midnight. I add that I just want her to know all of this because she was the one who urged me to follow through with my Chattanooga source, and for that, I thank her.

Once I'm done with the message, I copy it, paste it into an email, and send it without delay.

"What are you doing here?" a woman asks.

I quickly look toward the doorway. Julia Valentine fills the doorway wearing a long trench coat over a black business suit. Her outfit looks flawless, but her skin is blotchy and her eyes are crazed and glassy. It takes me a moment to fully process what she just asked.

"I'm sorry, but what are *you* doing here?" I ask. After all, I'm the girlfriend, and she's the fake fiancée —at least, that's what I've been told.

"I can't believe him," she grumbles as she sweeps out of the doorway. The sound of her heels beating the floor filters into Jasper's bedroom.

My heart is beating a mile a minute. My love bubble has been popped, and the relaxation I've discovered, obliterated. "What in the world?" I hop to my feet.

I want to follow her, but I'm too discombobulated. *What the hell just happened?* I gnaw on my bottom lip, still unable to figure out how to direct my feet. Then Julia yells about how Jasper has misled her and how he wasn't supposed to do what he has done to her father.

"We're losing everything by the second. How dare you?" she shouts.

Jasper says something in response. His face is dull, non-reactionary.

"I was falling in love with you. Do you even care about that?" she shouts.

I gasp and rub a hand over my heart.

He says something that includes my name.

Julia falls deathly silent then cries, "Fuck you Jasper! It won't work. What you did won't work!"

In a very cool, calm, and collected voice he says something else, and even though I try, I can't make out his words. I hear more footsteps—heavy, fast ones. Someone is running. Julia keeps yelling at someone to get out of her way.

"I know you love me too. We fucked!" she screams. "He fucked me good!" She sounds hysterical. And I think she saying that for my ears.

"You're lying!" he yells.

"No, I'm not lying, Holly Henderson! If you can hear me, I'm not lying, you cunt!"

I gasp. I was right. She's purposefully addressing me.

"Get her out of here!" Jasper roars. "If I see you again, it won't be advantageous for you."

I clench my stomach as my butt drops down on the foot of the bed. What just happened? And my heart...Does it ache? I rub my chest over my constricted heart. And then, Jasper appears in the doorway.

SEVEN

DOWN WITH THE VALENTINES

HOLLY HENDERSON

Jasper's eyes are wild with worry. "She was lying. I never touched her. I never wanted to."

"I believe you," I whisper. I really do. The fact that Julia was being spiteful is as clear as Saran Wrap.

Shoulders drooped from relief, Jasper pads over and sits down beside me. "Because I don't want her to topple all we've built together."

I swallow, frowning. I have one nagging thought that I would like addressed. "Why did she come to your bedroom?"

Grimacing like he's chewing on lemons, Jasper shakes his head. "I don't know. Julia has gotten into the habit of roaming freely through my home. I treated her as a friend so I could tolerate our arrangement."

I rest my hand on his thigh, and I can feel him take the tension out of it.

"It's okay, Jasper. As I said, I believe you."

He cups my chin and guides my mouth to his. Our lips embrace as our tongues, stroke and tangle and lips kiss sensually.

It's as if he's only barely able to pull away from my mouth when he whispers, "Thank you."

"You're welcome." My voice and head are airy.

His expression turns grave again. "His wealth has diminished. I drained him of massive amounts of his fortune."

My jaw drops. "But how? Valentine money is old and strong."

Jasper's brows draw closer together. "Thomas Valentine made a mistake when he didn't put his wealth in a stable trust."

"Right," I say, taking a moment to recall what I know about Thomas Valentine. He was a tycoon who'd taken a percentage of the oil industry out of Rockefeller's hands after the Antitrust Act of 1890 started the dismantling of Standard Oil. Jasper explains that when Thomas died, he split his fortune evenly among his descendants. Together, they agreed to sell their oil interest and split the profits among them. The Valentine fortune has become disjointed, which is a blessing or a curse, depending on who's telling the story. The blessing is that spreading their wealth limits their power, and the Valentines aren't the most moral individuals on earth. The curse is that as each decade passes, a new crop of Valentines find themselves broke. Conrad Valentine, Arthur's father, had left his son a diversified portfolio, and that had made Conrad and Arthur some of the strongest Valentines, at least until now.

"But how did you bankrupt him?" I ask.

"Methodically," Jasper says.

I wait for him to say more, but his lips are sealed. But my professional instincts want me to keep pushing for an answer.

"What's an example of *methodically*?" I ask.

I watch his jaw closely as he tightens it—but then, to my relief, he loosens it to sigh. And the type of sigh he makes indicates that he has surrendered to my question.

"Do you recall the demonstration I gave you the other day?" he asks.

I cock my head, trying to figure out what he's talking about. Unfortunately—or perhaps fortunately —all I can recall is the love we made.

"With the travel magazine?" he asks leadingly.

"Oh, yes. I remember." I recall his ability to remember whatever he reads.

"I was able to bankrupt him because I'm smarter than he is."

I watch him with a frown. For some reason, I can't take that explanation as the be-all and end-all. I can't be one of those women who hides in the shadows of her man's darkness.

"You said your actions were methodical," I say. "But they sure as hell couldn't have been legal."

Jasper keeps a straight face. "Was it legal when Arthur broke into your room and threatened you?"

I shift uncomfortably at the memory of Arthur's goon grinding my ass. "No."

"Is it legal for him to extort me and force me to marry his daughter and my sister to marry his son?"

I know where he's going with this line of questioning. I shake my head.

"Arthur's lust for power is his weakness, Holly. I took advantage of that. It didn't happen overnight. But I will say that I started destroying Valentine the moment my father was out of commission. Then you came into my life, and I had to struggle to remain patient while simultaneously speeding up the process."

I muse over the sped-up process. "Then if I hadn't come into your life, would you have married Julia?"

"Yes," he says without hesitation. "But I never could have loved her. And instead of bankrupting her father, I would've taken everything they had."

I take in his beautiful face. So this is the dangerous side of Jasper Blackstone that nobody wants to fuck with. "I'm still curious to know what you did to him."

Finally, Jasper looks at me with a hint of a satisfied smile. "I re-re-distributed his wealth..."

I narrow my eyes. "Humph?"

He chuckles as if amused by my response. "You're sexy when you do that."

I wave my finger at him. "Uh-uh. Don't seduce me now, Jasper Blackstone."

We smile at each other. It feels good to be solidly back where we were before Julia showed up acting like a crazy person.

"Since you're so beautiful and I'm in love with you, I'll tell you this. Thomas was a sanctimonious and hypocritical purist. The original will contained a clause stating that a descendant would have to pay restitution to the others in the amount of sixty percent of the original treasure if they brought shame on the family. Conrad broke the no-contest moral clause with the war-hero stunt he pulled."

That's right. Conrad Valentine claimed he was a World War II hero but wasn't.

I raise an eyebrow. "But why are they making him pay for it now and not then?"

Jasper presses his lips together, and once again, I understood what that meant.

"That's all you're willing to say?"

He nods graciously. "Yes. That's it."

At this point, I'm not sure I want to know more. The Valentines being broke isn't a story I want to break. But then an answer comes to mind.

"Did you incentivize one or more of the descendants to sue him?"

Looking into my eyes, Jasper keeps a straight face. There's no doubt he would make a world-class poker player.

I shrug, conceding. "Okay, then, we're done talking about it."

"We still have to be careful, though. Arthur isn't going down without a fight. And now Julia is completely on his side."

My eyebrows flick up as I sigh knowingly. "That's for sure."

We stare at each other. The longer our gazes

linger, the more my heart rate increases. Jasper's eyes veer down to my exposed cleavage. He wants sex. The next thing I know, his mouth is on mine, and we are kissing so hard, so intensely, that our teeth keep clacking together. He stops himself before ripping off my robe and spreading me on top of the bed.

"I want you now," he says with fervency, breathing heavily. "But we have to leave. Also there's been a change of plans."

Even though my head is still spinning, I'm able to ask, "What change of plans?"

"I'll tell you once we're out of here."

EIGHT

AMELIA'S WORDS

The maid brings my clothes, which includes my freshly washed panties and bra. Even my coat has a freshly laundered scent. She also gives me red cashmere earmuffs and a matching scarf, both courtesy of Jasper. We don't leave right away. Jasper has to take care of some last minute details. The big burly men, in black suits race up and down the hallways like there's a security breach of some kind in the apartment.

Jasper is right on time. As soon as I'm finished dressing, he walks into the bedroom and asks if I'm ready to leave. We can't delay our departure one minute later. On our way out, Jasper reveals the reason for all the excitement. Julia is being detained in one of the main elevators but will be released once we are in the sky and far away from the building.

"You know that's kidnapping, right?" I ask.

His left eyebrow raises keenly. "No. It's a mechanical difficulty."

I snort a chuckle as the cold air slams against my face. Jasper takes my hand, and we walk with our heads down to the helicopter. Thankfully, there's a break in the weather. Enough snow has fallen to cover the whole outside floor of the expansive terrace, but there isn't a drop of snow on the concrete. The entire terrace floor must be heated, a convenience that surely cost a lot of money. *Goodness, the man is richer than The King of Saudi Arabia.*

Jasper helps me into the aircraft, and sits beside me. Once we're both settled in our seats, he takes my hand again. His grip is tight, as if he's afraid I will somehow slip away from him. But Jasper doesn't have to worry about that. I'm not going anywhere.

THE HELICOPTER IS strong and mighty, but every now and then, it will become rattled by the weather. It happens again, and I focus on the pilot, who holds no tension in his shoulders. His confidence forces me to relax a bit. Also, Jasper holds me tighter to ease my worry. I figure if the aircraft drops from the sky, at least we will die together. Darkness is all around us and beneath us. About half an hour into the ride, I suss out we aren't on our way to Teterboro to board a private airplane, and ride it to Rhode Island. I would ask Jasper to enlighten me about his decision to ride it out in a helicopter, but I'm too exhausted to talk to have that conversation. So I yawn, and he holds me closer and kisses the top of my head.

***

"BABE," Jasper faintly calls. Then he says it louder.

I force my eyes open. My head is still groggy. Oh... I had fallen asleep.

Jasper unbuckles my seat belt and puts a soft kiss on my forehead. "Let's get you inside and into bed."

My entire body feels heavy. Despite being able to smell the ocean and feel the sort of moisture in the air that comes from being near the sea, I can hardly keep my eyes open. It's as if the last four days have come crashing down on me.

Jasper reminds me to keep my head down as we

disembark. His arm grips my waist as we walk off the helipad and across a short space of lawn. I lift my heavy eyes up to see the Blackstone mansion sitting in the distance, then we get into the back seat of a black car with dark-tinted windows. As soon as the car starts moving, I, rest my cheek against Jasper's chest and fall asleep again.

———————

THE FIRST THING I notice is the comfortable mattress and sheets beneath me. I stretch and squirmed as my body rises to full awareness. The sort of light that's muted by clouds sprays into the room. Next, I realize I'm naked. Finally, I become aware that I'm alone in bed.

I sit up fast with a gasp, but my heart stops pounding like thunder as my eyes connect with Jasper's. He's sitting in a chair by the window, shirtless and wearing his dress pants, watching me.

"Good morning," he says, looking as if he hasn't slept a wink.

I stretch like a cat rising from a nap. "Good morning," I say with a soft laugh. "How did I end up here?"

"I carried you in and put you to bed. I hope you don't mind."

"Not in the least." My gaze roams the room. We are in the cottage, and I'm in the same bed Jasper and I had made love in twice. "We didn't go to the main house..."

Jasper holds up a book. I crane my neck forward to get a better look. The cover is made of green silk fabric, and the edges of the pages are sprayed with gold paint.

"It's my mother's diary."

My entire face collapses into a frown. "Your mother's diary?"

He picks up the key that he brought with him from on top of the round table he's sitting next to and holds it up. "There's an antique table in the foyer of this cottage. This key opened a hidden drawer."

"Wow, were you up all night searching?" Just as I ask the question, I lose a handle on the portion of sheet I used to cover my breasts.

Jasper's eyes veer down to my exposed tits. His Adam's apple bobs as he swallows, and he frowns as he focuses on my face again. "Yes," he says quietly. Oddly, I feel as if I somehow annoyed him by showing him my breasts.

He drops the diary on the table, stands, and takes

off his pants, freeing an erection that's made of steel. His tapered torso and broad muscular chest makes my sex throb.

However, now I understand his facial expression. The first time I saw it was when I accidentally took his mother's space as my guest room and found him already in there, sitting in a chair. He glared at me as if he wanted to bang my brains out and scold me for doing something wrong. He looked at me in the same confounded way when he tried to bully me into signing a nondisclosure agreement. I recall how I stood up to him—how hot and bothered I'd become just from being near him. Like now... That's exactly how I'm feeling right this very second.

I smirk impishly as I cast my legs over the edge of the bed and trot to the bathroom. "Wait, I have to pee."

It's the most inopportune time for making love, but as usual, Jasper and I can hardly help ourselves. As I sit on the toilet, it seems as if my pee would last forever. *Did I drink that much liquid?* I expect my period to start in a few days, and my stomach feels bloated as if my cycle is just around the corner. Jasper and I have had so much sex without condoms —more without than with lately—that I won't be surprised if I end up pregnant. Interestingly enough,

I don't feel so bothered by that possibility. I've never given a thought to the sort of mother I would be. The idea of having children always scared the living daylights out of me. I always figured if it happened, then it would be God's will, and that was that, but I've definitely been testing divine will lately.

When I make it back to the bed, Jasper is lying on his back, his cock pointing up in the air.

"Sit on it, baby," he says.

That sounds so hot. I walk seductively to him, and his eyes burn with lust. I can tell by the way his cock tilts toward his belly that he's beyond excited. When I'm close enough, he reaches out and clenches my waist. What a strong man he is. Jasper pulls me to him. I straddle his body, and he sucks air as I slowly lower my sex down on his cock.

"Umm," he moans, eyes closed and head pressed back against the pillow.

Jasper shifts my hips against him. He moans, licking his lips. He shifts me faster and faster. Then his eyes open, and the fire in them sets my body aflame. He is beyond turned on—the next thing I know, he sits up, curls an arm around me, and flips me onto my back.

"Oh, baby," he keeps saying as he moves in and out of me.

I'm purposely quiet as he makes delicious love to me. I want to hear him. The sex we're having now is totally for him, and it was okay. However, Jasper's cock is a thing of magic. I cling to him tighter as he speeds up the pace, making me feel...

My mouth opens and I sigh as...

I squeeze a handful of bed linens as...

"Ah..." I cry out as pure pleasure spreads through my sex.

"Fuck," Jasper roars as he shivers with an orgasm. When his body stills, he trails kisses along the side of my face. "Thank you for that," he whispers, and our tongues dive into each other's mouths.

"So..." I say while kissing.

"So..." he whispers back.

"What were you saying about a diary before... you know?"

He chuckles, and I join him.

JASPER and I sit next to each other in bed as he reads portions of Amelia's diary. The first entry is about how Sally Preacher, Amelia's personal maid, had given her the book for her birthday. Amelia wrote that Randolph never would have condoned it.

He was too worried that people would find out who she really was.

"Last night, he threatened to kill me and my son again. He's a monster, not a man. I hate him. I hate him enough to kill him. I want vengeance," Jasper reads. He looks at me. The flash of anger in his eyes is quickly quelled by whatever he feels when he looks at me.

I raise my eyebrows at Jasper. "Wow, she had no love for him." I turn on my side, and I can tell he's trying to avoid looking at my tits again. "By the way, was the FBI able to confirm her kidnapping?"

Jasper swallows and nods.

I reach up to run my fingers gently down the side of his face. "I'm sorry, my love."

He captures my wrist and kisses the back and palm of my hand. "What did you call me?" He smiles just a little.

"My love."

"I like that. Call me that often, please."

I felt my face beaming as I repeat "my love" until we kiss tenderly. I sigh as our lips part.

"Babe, we have to focus. I don't know if keeping you with me was the best idea." His eyes do what they've been trying to avoid doing—he glares at my tits. "I can't stop wanting to be inside you." His finger flicks my nipple, and then his hot mouth comes down over the tip of it.

Orgasmic sensations seize my core. "I catch your drift," I whisper, eyes falling behind my head. *I so catch his drift.*

"All right." He rolls out of bed suddenly and is on his feet. "Let's get out of here."

I felt my eyes grow wide. "Where are we going?"

He opens the book to a certain page and flips it around to face me. All I see is Amelia's cursive hand-writing. Her script is elegant, practiced.

"We're going to visit my grandparents and ask them why they took the money."

My mouth falls open. "What?"

"My father paid them off." He rotates the book so that the pages face him and read, "Mama and Daddy don't love me anymore. They were poisoned by Randolph's money. They sold me to him. If it wasn't for my son and the other children, I would kill myself, but they need me."

Mouth agape, I clutch the pearls I'm not wearing. "Oh my God, Jasper. I don't know what else to say."

"*Oh my God* is good enough."

NINE
BINGO
HOLLY HENDERSON

I put on my second shoe, and as soon as my foot hits the floor, I look up at Jasper, who has just gotten off the phone with the helicopter pilot. The two of them are planning the logistics of our flight off the property. The weather has kicked up again, and Jasper doesn't want to put our lives in jeopardy, but he wants to get out of Dodge the fastest way possible.

An uneasy feeling has been brewing within me ever since Jasper announced we were on our way to have a talk with his grandparents. I sigh forcefully. "My love, you're a thinker. Have you thought this through?"

"No, but I'm tired of thinking it through. How about I let raw emotion guide me for a change."

I shake my head, wondering if he realizes what

he just said. That he's not sounding like himself at all. But maybe he isn't supposed to sound like himself. His whole world was turned upside down the moment he learned his mother had been kidnapped. I can't imagine being in his shoes.

Jasper's cell phone rings and he excuses himself before walking out of the bedroom to take the call. "Yeah," I hear him faintly say as he barrels down the short hallway.

Wow... This all seems so surreal. I turn to really study the bed Jasper and I just made love on top of. I can still feel him inside me. If only we could still be in bed, sexing the day away. I love the way his skin feels on my skin. I love hearing his deep voice so close to my ear when we talk as we cuddle. Then before an hour is up, he'll rise again and move inside me. I'll sigh on first thrust.

"Holly," Jasper calls.

I jump. His voice interrupting my fantasy.

I shoot to my feet. "What is it?"

"Come here, babe."

I quickly grab my coat and purse and rush into the living room. Jasper is sitting on the sofa, looking at the screen of his laptop which sits on his lap.

He turns to look at me with his eyes narrowed. "What's this?"

I scowl at the screen as I sit beside him. It's an article from *JWR*, and it includes all the details I fed Kylie, who was careful to make sure that she only used information from my fake sources.

I close my eyes as I shake my head. I'm more heartbroken than angry. "I'm so sorry. I forgot to tell you that I fed Kylie the fake story yesterday."

"You actually did it?"

I nod. "I said I would."

"But you should've informed me first."

I tighten my mouth, avoiding saying what I'm thinking. Before our current situation, I would have told Jasper to go to hell. I did what I wanted, when I wanted. But he's the one who told me about Kylie's dishonest acts. I owe him a strong degree of allegiance.

"I apologize, my love. Things went so fast last night that it slipped my mind. I should've told you before I did it. I was just so angry."

His frown doesn't ease, but that's okay. At least I feel better about getting that off my chest.

"It's fine," he mutters. "We can actually use this to our benefit. But there's something else."

"What is it?"

"Bryn and Katie escaped from the compound. They're in Nashville with Dale and Zach."

My jaw slackens. "Bryn is at the compound?"

I sigh gravely. "Oh no. It must've been jarring for Katie to walk into a great big house and unexpectedly run into her twin sister."

Jasper falls back against the sofa and wipes his palms over his face. "I considered how painful it could be for both of them, but I concluded the impact would be the same whether or not we were there. I had to prioritize. What I hadn't properly taken into account was how capable my sister is at creating chaos." Jasper's hands fall onto the sofa. "Or maybe I'm tired of it all."

He looks so miserable, less like a demigod and more like a mere mortal. I stroke his strong thigh, hoping to bring him comfort. "Don't be so hard on yourself. I've never met someone who had so many irons in the fire. And yet you manage them all with such ease and expertise."

Jasper studies me as if he's been barely listening. "What if I give up?" he says, his expression the picture of pure misery.

"Give up what?"

"I've been holding this family together for as long as I can remember. All for a secret that could destroy us." His eyes narrowed even more as he tilts his head to the side. "And I've been asking myself why Arthur hasn't come out with it. I'm decimating him right now, yet he hasn't struck back."

I grunt thoughtfully. Jasper was watching me intently. Perhaps he can see me thinking. He just said something that makes a hell of a lot of sense, and my professional instincts are putting the pieces together.

"Remember when we showed Kat a photo of your father and she said she knew him as Arthur?"

Jasper's eyes narrow some more. Then his mouth opens as if he's about to take the words right out of my mouth. I pause, waiting to see if that's exactly what's about to happen.

Knock, knock, knock.

Jasper and I jump.

"Be out in a second," Jasper calls and then intensifies his focus on me. "He can't do it without implicating himself."

I smile wryly. It's such a relief to be in love with a very sexy and extremely intelligent man. "Yep."

TEN
BRONWYN'S STORY

24 Hours Ago

Finally, the helipad on the west lawn lights up signaling Holly and Jasper's impending arrival. I've been waiting all morning to see them. I have two words to say to Holly, "Thank you." I knew when I invited her to our home to find something, anything on my family that will provide me with an answer to a question I didn't even know to ask, she would get results.

My father is dead. I say that often out loud just to bask in how that feels. Randolph Blackstone is dead. Not an ounce of me misses that wretched motherfucker. He's always been creepy. Every memory I have of him makes my skin crawl. For the longest time, he had been nothing more to me than a man who came and went. Then, one day, it occurred to me that he was my father.

Up until I became a teenager, Randolph ignored me, outside of needing me to dress up in uncomfortable buttoned-up clothes to play the part of his rich, cute, and obedient daughter. But when I hit puberty, the old creepy man couldn't keep his eyes to himself. He would stare at my body, and I'm positive he didn't realize he was doing it. He seemed to be possessed by something lascivious. That thing inside him had taken him over. For three years my father watched me in that creepy way. Remembering it now makes my stomach turn.

At thirteen, I could feel Randolph's strange energy concentrate on me whenever I showered. I could pinpoint the location from which it came. One morning, through the wet glass, I stared at a white ceramic vase that held fake pink and white roses. Eyes narrowed, I focused on the back panel of the cabinet, past a pink petal. And there it was—a tiny hole a little larger than pin-sized. Following my instincts, I grabbed a towel, wrapped it around me, and tugged at the white cabinet. I gasped at how easily it opened. Cold, untempered air washed over me, cooling my wet skin as I tiptoed into a dark space with concrete floors. A foul odor lingered in the air—like stinky armpits and loud cologne. Then I saw another door. Without an ounce of fear, I opened it and stepped into a dingy hallway. That is when I first discovered the tunnels, which are a web of hallways that run through the house and even underground.

On the day I discovered the tunnels I knew I wasn't crazy. Someone had been watching me. I also, knew I could never feel safe in my own house. At first, I thought it might have been one of the butlers or another male servant, watching me shower, but the only man who had steadily undressed me with his eyes was Randolph.

Later that evening, I arrived at the dinner table early and he was already seated. He'd seen me before I could duck out of the room. I hated being alone with him and tried to avoid it whenever possible.

"Girl," Randolph called, waving me over to where he sat at the head of the table. That's what he called me, Girl.

I froze, my feet warned me not to go. But his thin fingers wouldn't stop waving me to him. How was I supposed to know that I should've taken off running the opposite direction anyway? I went to him. I stood petrified as his thin fingers came down on my shoulders and massaged my tiny bones. My stomach became nauseated. I was positive it was his scent I smelled in the small room behind the cabinet. He seemed pleased to be touching me as beads of sweat glistened on his forehead.

"You've grown into a striking creature." He pulled out the chair next to his. "Sit beside your father." His voice sounded creepy.

"Run," a small voice inside me screamed. But, I was taught to obey him, so I sat. I kept thinking, why is he still touching me in that horrible way. Then his clammy hands found their way to my pubescent breasts, purposely rubbing one of my small nipples. I remember breathing heavily. I felt paralyzed and even more sick to my stomach. He wrapped his hand around my wrist, and I believe he was about to make me touch him when...

"Father," Jasper roared as he stormed into the dining room.

Randolph instantly stopped touching me. But he didn't startle and jump like I had. I felt as if I was caught doing something terribly wrong. But Randolph remained as cool as a cucumber.

Then Jasper grabbed the top of a chair on the opposite side of the table, pulled it up and back, and slammed the legs on the floor. The sound made me shudder.

"Bryn sits here." Jasper glared at Randolph, daring their father to challenge him. Then he turned his tapered eyes to her. "Bryn, sit here." His tone was less ominous with me but still very severe.

I'll never forget the Jasper I saw at that moment. Jasper wasn't like other teenage boys that I had come across from time to time. He kept a rigid exercise regime that made him built like a world class athlete. He commanded the world around him with grace and dominance. To me, Jasper was king—he was god.

I hopped up out of my chair as fast as I could and sat in the safe seat. Eventually Randolph left the dinner table before everyone arrived. He always preferred to eat in his parlor. Not until he had fell very ill had I seen his parlor. The red leather and dark wood furniture, the faint smell of tobacco, the room reminded me of a gin joint, which were rooms in the days of prohibition where people would sneak off to consume their illegal alcohol.

On the night, Jasper saved me from Randolph at the dinner table, I asked him if I could shower in his bathroom. He studied me, frowning as he usually did, but didn't ask why I didn't want to use my own shower. Instead, he gave me permission to take a shower wherever the hell I wanted. Jasper's bathroom was safer. Jasper was the safest person in my world. However, the next day, Jasper looked me in the eye and informed me that from that moment onward, I could use my bathroom and any other bathroom in the house.

"It's safe," he said.

We didn't have to discuss what "safe" meant. We both knew.

Finally, the helipad lights flash green, signaling that the helicopter will touch down in less than a minute. I smiled. I'd been doing that more easily recently—smiling. Randolph is dead! Of course, he had tried to control me from the grave by making me marry Carter Valentine. Carter and I are friends but nothing more. Our fathers had to have known that Carter isn't into it. Carter is asexual.

Dale Rumor is the man I love. After my first and only year of college, he and I had lost contact with each other. We weren't in love back then, but we had sex whenever he would come to my dorm room. However, three years ago, I traveled to Washington, DC, to play the good daughter of the Blackstone clan during a fundraiser. Randolph was being recognized as the donor who had given the most money to whatever fake charity was hosting the event. Dale happened to be there. Seeing him again reminded me of how much I loved my freedom during that year of college. During that trip, Sally Preacher, whose job it was to keep a close eye on me, loosened her leash so that I could have "normal" relations with someone my age. Dale had taken me to his hotel room, and we had fucked all day and all night. Ever since that weekend in Washington, we've been seeing each other.

Every now and then, Dale would visit the mansion and enter my room through the tunnels. We'd spend days making love. I knew to keep him a complete secret, I couldn't even let Nigel, the butler —who had become like a surrogate father to me— know about my trysts with Dale, even though Nigel was carrying on his own affair with Amelia. Plus, there was so much secret loving going on around the mansion that no one paid attention to relationships outside their own.

It was Dale who had come up with a genius plan to fake our disappearance. At first, I told him it was stupid, but he insisted it would give us time to get as far away from my insane family as possible. On the night of the Christmas party, Jasper had lured Dale to the cigar room and had him thrown off the grounds by his bruisers. I wanted to go smash Jasper's head in for doing that, but instead, when Dale found his way back to my room through the tunnels, we made a plan to get away from everybody. The next morning, I got lucky as hell, Randolph died, and I grew wings. I escaped the mansion and met Dale at the airport.

We faked our disappearance in LA. We planted our blood in Dale's car and left the engine running on the 101 Freeway. Then Dale, a licensed and trained pilot, flew us to Aruba. Two days later, Jasper found us, even though we had done a thorough job of covering our trail. Jasper has the ability to think three or four steps ahead of the average person. He's brilliant in that way. I still don't know exactly how he found us—he's not telling.

However, Jasper liked the idea of the two of us being missing. He said that he was on the tail end of destroying Arthur Valentine and he didn't want his family accessible for Valentine to strike back.

Dale and I had been on the beach, lying on lounge chairs and sucking down cocktails, when Jasper had told us that. Jasper had on a spiffy pair of trousers and a white shirt with the sleeves folded to above his elbows, which was how he always wore his shirts. I recall looking into his mirrored sunglasses, thinking how out of place my brother looks on this gorgeous and relaxing beach. He didn't know how to unwind. For him, life was solving one crisis after another, and there I was, making another fire for him to put out. Regardless, the day was cloudy, the humidity high, and the temperature eighty degrees. The day was made even more perfect when Jasper assured me that I was indeed free from the obligation of marrying Carter.

Since then Jasper has been straight with us. He's told us about Holly's findings. Amelia was not my mother. I thought I'd be angry when I learned that, but instead I felt relieved.

Finally, the helicopter appears and hovers over its landing spot.

"Bryn," Nigel, the house butler calls before I can run out to meet the new arrivals.

I turn to see him behind me, walking fast down the long hallway.

"A message for you," he says, handing me a slip of folded paper.

After I secure the slip of paper, he walks away.

Frowning curiously, I unfold the note and read it.

1 Hour Later

Our conversation starts with a simple question.

"Can we talk?" I ask.

Katie, that's her name, stares at me as if she's seeing a ghost.

Earlier, after I finished reading the note, I looked out the window to see her disembark. She was me, and I am her. My insides felt as if they were compressing as I watched William greet her and walk her into our Greenwich, Connecticut manor. My eyes filled with tears. But why? I wasn't happy or sad, I felt numb. I always feel numb. However, if that was the case, then why the tears?

From JC—

I'M sorry I couldn't make it. Something came up. You'll soon meet Katie. She is Asher and your twin sister. Holly uncovered her existence, and I sent her to the manor to keep her safe. I'm sorry to spring this on you, Bryn. Please be courteous to Katie. She is our family.

—JC

That's what the note said. It was neatly hand written by Nigel. I've come to loathe how impersonal

Jasper can be at times. Although, he couldn't have just called me. Our cellphones don't work at this property. It's a place where no one comes in or goes out unnoticed. The perimeter is under twenty-four hour surveillance. However, Randolph is the one who bought and built this estate and therefore there is always a slippery and slimy way to get in and out.

But Katie is looking at me and I really think she's been shocked into speechlessness. So, I figure I should get right to the point.

"I have some questions to ask you." I take a breath. There goes that feeling again. The backs of my eyes burn and I'm fighting the urge to cry when I say, "About our mother."

Hours Later

I have learned that Katie grew up in a house with other girls in Chattanooga, Tennessee. She never attended school and couldn't read hardly at all until she escaped to New York City. Once she got a taste of learning, she never stopped.

We sit in the gray fiber high chairs by the picture windows. A plush garden with marble statues of naked females. I heard *A Midsummer Night's Dream* was inspiration for the garden, but I don't see the correlation. The play took place in the forest and those naked women should probably be fairies. That's what I'm thinking during this moment of silence.

But there's something else burning my brain. It's one question that I think I should ask. "How did you escape the house for good?"

For a moment Katie seems distracted by her own thoughts. But then she stiffens, adjusts in her seat, and says, "A girl named Alexia saved me."

Katie tells the story of how the girl across the street, Alexia, had become her only friend and the only person in the outside world who knew she existed. The girl would bring her food. However, Alexia would do all sorts of drugs. Katie never touched drugs because if she went back into the house high, they would have known she had been sneaking out.

One day, Katie went to the woods and found Alexia gagging, eyes rolling back in her head, and frothing at the mouth. Katie knew to call 911 because she had heard Bam tell Sissy—the woman he relied on to run all his errands and talk to the women when problems arose—to drop a girl off at the bus stop and dial that number if something happened.

"That sounds awful," I say, unthinkingly.

"It's all awful," she whispers as if she's being haunted by that existence at this very moment.

She goes on to explain how she had found all of this extra strength to pick Alexia up and practically dragged her to that bus stop Bam had referred to. Katie then found Alexia's cell phone on her and called 911. The ambulance came. She knew it was best to just go home, but one of the EMTs, a young guy, invited her to ride along. Something about his eyes and her friend's condition made her go with them.

When they arrived at the hospital, she sat in the waiting room, afraid that Bam would show up. He used to punish them by whipping them with a rod then starving them for a week. She'd endured the punishment once before. Although she could tolerate it, she hated suffering through it. The first person who sat beside her in the waiting room to talk to her was the EMT with the kind eyes. She was intimidated and scared of his maleness, but he kept asking her questions about what had happened. It got to the point where he had to ask her to please look him in the eyes. She hadn't noticed she wasn't doing that. When their eyes met, she saw something different about him. He wasn't the sort of pig who would come to the house and study the women as if he were shopping for a good time. He urged her to tell him the truth about who she was and why she'd been in those woods.

She told the EMT that she couldn't tell him, or she'd get in trouble. He took her to a private space in the hospital and convinced her that there was no one there but the two of them. This was the time to confess. All she could say was that she lived in a house with very bad people, and they didn't know she was missing. Then the EMT got a call on his radio, telling him that the police and the girl's father were ready to speak to Katie.

"I grabbed his arm, holding it tight. There was something in me that wanted to fight for my life, so I just gushed," Katie says.

She told him that she didn't have a father and that she lived in a house where women were forced to have sex with men for money. She had never known her real parents, had never gone to school, and didn't even have a real name.

The EMT believed her and radioed back that he couldn't locate Katie. He gave her his address and asked if she knew how to find it. She was forced to admit that she couldn't read letters, only numbers.

"I probably should've been embarrassed, but I wasn't even normal enough to get it. He told me to not leave that room. It was the office of a doctor friend who was out for the day. The EMT came back to get me, and we've been together ever since. He's my boyfriend, Zach. He was an EMT then, but now he's a resident doctor at New York Presbyterian."

Zach had taught Katie how to read at a twelfth-grade level, and three years later, she attended adult school. She eventually received her GED. But they had to leave Tennessee to keep her in hiding. She had two names—Faye and Eve. If someone were to come looking for Eve, she and Zach would know that her old life had found them, and they needed to drop their current life and go somewhere and build another one.

"But that was before Zach had become a surgical resident. He can't just leave and I don't want to live without him. I never told him that Holly called me asking to speak to Eve. I didn't want to burden him with that."

It's the time of day when the light of day is noticeably changing. The atmosphere around the white statues, which have soaked up as much of the sunlight as they could, is duller. I think snow has finished falling for the day. The weather, Katie, and my numb existence provokes some obscure desire inside me. But the longer I sit with Katie, and we've been talking for quite a long time, the more that need takes shape.

"And you knew Randolph?" I ask.

"I guess so," she says. "He's dead, right?"

My insides tighten as I nod. Oh, the anger soaring through me... It's a miracle that I am containing it. "Did he ever touch you?" Because she wouldn't have had a Jasper around to protect her.

Katie shakes her head. "Beth would always send me outside before he could see me."

That's it.

That's her.

I know it.

I'm practically sitting on the edge of my seat. "Beth?"

"I think..." Katie drops her eyes to look at her lap. She tugs nervously at a loose string at the hem of her sweater. "She's our mother."

My mouth is caught open and breaths are coming slow and deep. "Where is she?" My voice is barely audible.

When Katie looks up she looks alarmed by me. I

know why. My tears rolling. My heart feels like it's standing on the precipice of something big, and if my need is not fulfilled, it will stop beating.

"She's a maid," Katie whispers.

"Where?" I ask in desperation.

"Nashville."

Suddenly, the door pushes open and Katie and I jump startled. It's Dale. His hair is messy, face gaunt, eyes dull and his travel bag and laptop are slung over his shoulder. "Bryn, I'm getting the fuck..." His eyes shift between me and Katie several times. "What the hell?"

I GIVE Dale a quick rundown of almost everything Katie has shared with me. He doesn't need to know the hard parts. However, while I'm speaking, Katie frowns at her cell phone. I'm watching her fingers go to settings and then my eyes veer up to her disappointed face when she finally realizes that there is no mobile service at this house. At least not for us.

"I can't reach Zach," she says, trying again to call him.

"Who's Zach," Dale asks.

I've got my eye on him. He's giving me frantic

energy. Also, the wheels in his brain have been turning from the moment I said that Kat is my twin sister separated at birth.

"He's my boyfriend," Katie says.

With a burst of energy Dale sits up tall. His palms are facing us. The entire shift from bending over with his forearms resting on his knees while occasionally tapping his right foot to how he's sitting now, signals an abrupt change in the present situation.

"Bryn, we've been presented with an opportunity here," he starts.

My eyebrows pull. Dale has a way of leading me down dark paths that will eventually turn out bad. He goes on about our TV series deal with Make TV, and that we have an opportunity to get some interest in the story before the pilot is shot and aired.

I'm shaking my head but there's no way I can say no to him. "We can't leave."

He grins, which is something he hasn't done since we left Aruba. Jasper rubs him the wrong way and vice versa. Dale would've been perfectly okay with hiding out at a mansion of this size and scale with everything we could ever want at our fingertips, if Jasper wasn't in charge.

"You know Nate, the groomer?"

I answer by intensifying my frown.

"He owes me a favor."

Apparently, Dale gave Nate the last of his marijuana, which made Nate grateful enough to arrange trail following horses to take him, and now us, to the outskirts of the property. Nate also has a cellphone on a network that gets shitty service, however, Dale was able to order a cab to take him into the city where he planned to take the train the La Guardia. But now, that plan has changed since Katie and I are sneaking off the estate with him, and flying to Nashville to see our mother.

ELEVEN
THE FRIENDLY SKIES
HOLLY HENDERSON

Back to the Present

He could definitely be president, I think as I watch Jasper through the small round window of the aircraft. His strides are long and sure as he strolls toward the ramp. He was just having a conversation, standing with the pilot on one side of him and his security chief on the other. There was no doubt which of the men was in charge: the man in the middle, Jasper Blackstone.

For a second, our eyes connect. I smile at him. He winks, and that small acknowledgement makes me feel all warm and gooey inside. Sometimes it's hard to believe that Jasper is only thirty-three—he carries himself like a man ten to fifteen years older.

But on rare occasions when he smiles, he looks his age or even younger. I can't settle on which version of him I like most. When making love, I certainly prefer the man. No boy can bring my body such divine pleasure. Also, it's the man who pays attention to how I feel at all times. However, the boy—he smiles, winks at me, and occasionally finds humor in my attempt to lighten his mood. The boy will say that he wants to runaway with me, and ditch all of his heavy responsibilities. One day we will runaway. It'll just be him and I making love on the soft sands of a tropical beach. Then we'll sip cocktails and do nothing but watch the sunset while holding hands.

I had forgotten to put my phone in Airplane mode, and now it's ringing in my purse. I quickly fish it out of my bag and see that it's Kylie calling. Her sources must've been followed up on by another news outlet. She knows I fed her false information.

I'm not ready yet so I send her call straight to voicemail. I would have loved to hash it out with her, but now isn't the best time. Plus, I'm still upset about how she'd tried to use me, not once, but now twice. If I had validated all of my sources, and if what I sent her had been true, she would've stolen that story right out from under me. No real friend would do that.

I grunt dully, struck by the thought that the nature of our association is officially over. I mean, I can't even trust her professionally. She steals stories and employs underhanded tactics to get what she wants. I've been trying to figure out why she would operate that way. She's not all phony articles and subpar reporting. Kylie has broken some major stories in the past. Every reporter gets frustrated with having to validate our sources when we know deep in our bones that what we've written, what we're ready to present is true. But sometimes a story can fall apart after sources have been checked.

"Is everything okay?" Jasper asks, sitting down beside me.

I startle a little, I've been sitting with my eyes closed thinking. But now that I smell him and his energy showers me like a meteor storm, thoughts of Kylie disintegrate into nothingness. I nestle up against Jasper's strong arm. "All's well now that you're here."

He stretches his arm around me and kisses my forehead. "What was bothering you before I showed up?"

Of course Jasper would ask me that. It's one of the few ways in which we are similar. So I tell him about the call from Kylie and what I plan to do about it.

"You know you don't owe her an explanation," he says.

"No, I didn't know that," I say in a small voice, frowning.

"Unless you still want a relationship with her."

I shake my head. "She burned that bridge to the ground."

He nods, giving a tight-lipped smile. He likes my answer. Although, I wasn't trying to please him, even though I'm glad I had.

"So..." I sigh, squeezing his powerful thigh.

His eyebrows go up. "So?"

"So what's the plan after we arrive in Nashville?"

Jasper is staring at my hand on his thigh. "I don't know," he whispers thickly.

Hmm... Is my touch getting him all hot and bothered? I test my theory by raising my hand a few inches higher. Jasper skips a breath. He's just as horny as I suddenly am.

"You don't?" I purr, stroking his thigh, purposely not touching his package.

"I really don't. I know what to do, but..." He lifts his hips so his bulge can reach my hand.

I catch his drift and grab a handful of Jasper Blackstone's solidness. *There's no stopping me now.* Then two flight attendants board, and that cools me down.

Jasper winks at me.

"Hello, Mr. Blackstone," one of the ladies says.

They both examine me as if I am an exotic creature. But after a few seconds of awkward pause, they greet me just as cheerily. They already know my name, which makes me feel as if I deserve to be riding on a private airplane with the handsome billionaire I've fallen in love with. Next, Joseph, Jasper's security, boards the craft. He takes a seat in the chair nearest the cockpit.

I put my mouth to Jasper's ear. "If we aren't going to be alone, then why did you encourage me?"

He grins naughtily. "I wanted to see how far you were willing to go."

I snort a chuckle. "Do you think I've gotten this far in life by being afraid?"

Jasper turns his head slightly and studies me.

I unbuckle his pants. Nothing is going to stop me, and he will see it in how determined my hands are. I unzip.

"Joe—privacy," Jasper orders. I had his cock in my hand. "Now." He thumbs over his shoulder as my hand goes up and down his beautiful cock. "Attendants—in the kitchen."

The flight attendants sail past us, careful to not look at me getting on my knees.

"Babe..." He rests his head back against the soft leather seat. "What are you doing?" His protest sounds feeble.

My mouth can't wait a second longer. "Um..." I moan, the soft skin of his hard cock against my tongue. Jasper hand grabs two handfuls of my hair as my mouth bobs up and down. His silky saltiness fills my taste buds. I have never enjoyed giving blowjobs, but hearing him suck air as my tongue rounds his fat tip makes me hot. "Um..." My mouth works faster. Teeth restrained, I stuff him deeper down my throat.

"Oh, baby," he says breathlessly. "Yes."

I suck his tip, swirling my tongue around his slippery head, and then sink him deep into my throat again.

"Oh shit..." He shivers. "Oh!"

I feel his warm milk in my mouth. I have never swallowed before, but every part of me wants so much more of Jasper in my body. So I drank every drop of him.

Jasper breathes heavily as his vitals stabilize. "Damn, baby." He stuffs his softened cock back into his pants then guides me to my feet to set me on his lap. His tongue plunges into my mouth, seizing mine. My head spins like a top as we kiss. I long to have his manhood inside me, but he has given me all he has for the moment. It will be a while before Jasper is up and ready again—at least an hour.

"We're scheduled for takeoff in five," the captain announces.

I chuckle in Jasper's mouth.

"I want you so bad right now," he whispers fervently.

"You came fast," I say.

His eyebrows flit up. "I know. I was too turned on to last. I wanted to come as soon as I was in your mouth."

I smolder, looking into his eyes. "Then let's do it again soon."

"You'd better believe it." He grabs my hair, tilts my head back, and kisses me deeply.

We kiss strong but not long. Once his lips abandon mine, he used the call button to let the captain know we are ready to take to the skies. The flight attendants are back, smiling as though Jasper hadn't cleared them out of the cabin so that I could receive him in my mouth. I picture what I swallowed of him, in my body being digested, feeding my cells.

For the moment, I am him and he is me. Not even a small part of me could be embarrassed about that.

The flight attendants close the doors and let us know the breakfast, which has been prepared by Chef Bartholomew, will be served once we reach cruising altitude.

I look at Jasper with excitement. "Really? Chef Bart?"

"He's in the kitchen," Jasper says and instructs the flight attendant to bring my computer.

I gasp in surprise. "My computer? I left it in my hotel room?"

"I had someone collect your things, if you don't mind."

"It's a little too late to mind," I say with a laugh. "But no, Mister-Handle-Everything-Sexy-Control-Freak, I don't mind. Thank you, actually."

"You're welcome," he replies.

I kiss him on his cheek and then take my MacBook Pro from the flight attendant. Jasper lets me know that as soon as we reach cruising altitude, I will have Internet connection. I take a moment to recall the early days, when I would have done anything not to connect to his Internet service. Boy, we have come a long way.

Soon the aircraft is darting down the runway.

When we reach cruising altitude, I power up my computer. Bart has personally served us strawberry crepes with scrambled eggs and croissants with various kinds of jams. I eat alone. Jasper has joined the security guy in a private room to discuss their business. It has been two days since I drank a good cup of coffee, so the flight attendants keep my cup filled to the brim with a hot, delicious Salvadoran light roast. I have hundreds of emails to answer, many from Kylie but, surprisingly, none from Rachel. Kylie might have not been a real friend, but Rachel is. I create a new message with the subject *Question* and address it to Rachel.

I think for a moment about what to say. In actuality, I walked out on my job. Granted, when she showed me those fake photos of Jasper and Julia, she was on the verge of trying to convince me that it was in my best interest to quit the job she offered me. She wouldn't have had to pull my arm. A small smile comes to my lips as I figure out exactly what to write.

Hi Rach,

You were going to fire me, right?

I send that email. Once that's done, I look at stories that a few editors wonder if I'm interested in investigating. To my surprise, there's a message from

Dennis Thompson of JWR, asking if I had investigated the story regarding the Blackstones.

I quickly type out a reply.

No, I haven't. Why do you ask?

My eyebrows raise and hold when I see that Rachel has replied to me right away.

I would never fire you, Holly Henderson. However, I was not going to officially hire you. As long as you are involved with Mr. Blackstone I think it's for the best.

I blurt a laugh. Rachel certainly has a way with words. She managed to keep our bridge intact while basically saying that my unsavory boyfriend is why she doesn't want me on her team. But she's right. I will always be on Jasper's side. If she wants to run stories on him, then they better be favorable or else the unfavorable stories will be conflict of interest as far as I'm concerned. I want to type that she should be worried about her own position if she feels the need to keep me off her team because she doesn't like the new owner of the station.

Just asking. Thanks for confirming. Good luck.

I'm happy with that response. It's gracious and I'm not interested in burning a bridge with her either.

Her next reply comes faster.

Good luck to you too. I hope we can remain friends.

I reply:

Always.

She sends another quick message:

And perhaps sometimes colleagues.

I screw my mouth thoughtfully. At the moment, Rachel isn't aware that she's involved with a journalist who is the embodiment of professional cyanide. The first reply that comes to me is, *Perhaps.* But I can't think of her as a friend and colleague if I don't lead her to the truth.

I type:

Call Dennis at JWR and ask about Kylie's latest story.

I don't press send. I'm not sure it's my place to out Kylie, especially since I set her up. Jasper trusted me with details from his investigation on Kylie. I'm afraid that if I warn Rachel, Kylie's actions may grow too big to not bring charges against her.

I delete my last message and write:

Perhaps.

And that's how we leave it.

The more stories I research, the more I begin to understand what kind of conundrum I'd find myself in. I don't have the motivation to travel from city to city, chasing down sources. Perhaps, in my case, being in love is equivalent to professional suicide. I want to always be near Jasper. I want to see him every day. I want morning sex with him and afternoon kisses. I'm sure I can have all of that and be a journalist too—I just have to remain local.

I ponder the idea of working for a magazine. The thought fizzles away just as fast as it comes. I'm not in to it. I start a new document and write down all the secrets I've been hiding deep inside myself. First, I enjoy being a journalist, but it's not the writing that I like—I relish the act of discovery, questioning my sources, and painting the big picture. I love finding the whole truth. Using the techniques I learned at the university to write articles has always been a chore. I've even hired screenwriters—since they are trained to find the action in a story—to help me write my two books. My editor has been on me to produce a third manuscript, but frankly, I don't have another book in me.

Are you sure, Holly? I close my eyes to deeply ponder that question. I am more than sure.

So I open the email from my publisher and type:

I don't have a book in me right now. Sorry. Good luck.

And that's it. My quest for my next big story has

officially ended, even though I'm on the precipice of a really big story with Jasper Blackstone.

Investigator, I type into the document I just created. I follow it up with *What do I want to be? I like investigation.*

My mind is racing when Jasper walks out of the room he's been in with the security guy. It never gets old to not see him and then all of a sudden there he is. I'm dazzled by him right now.

"Sorry to leave you alone for so long," he says.

He makes me smile like this too—all warm and fuzzy inside. "It's no problem. I kept myself busy."

As he sits, my left hand connects with his right hand and our fingers enfold. My heart goes pitter-patter and that's when I'm hit by a disturbing sense of clarity. At the moment, I want nothing at all but Jasper. Quickly, I pull my hand out of his and stare at the document on my computer screen.

Jasper had already seen it before I could close it. "What are you writing, babe?"

I can't explain that I'm too in love with him to think about my career. I can't tell him that I'm afraid of being one of those women that was interesting before the greatest man in the world fell in love with her, and who at some point forgot who she was and lost her flair.

I shrug, figuring I should take a stab at having this conversation with him. Jasper is sensible and wise, maybe he has the answers I can't figure out right now. "I don't know. I was thinking about doing something else."

"Doing something else with what?"

"My life."

"Ah, I see," he says, sounding relieved. Then he squeezes my hand. "We haven't discussed our future together, but there's no better time than now to do it. Do you agree?"

I'm both elated and terrified by the conversation he's starting. The scared little girl in me wants to run away from the talk and hide in her row house in Philadelphia. The grown woman wants to brace herself for what is sure to be a life-changing chat. I let my grown-up lead and nod stiffly.

"I don't want to be away from you," he says.

My throat and heart tightens. I can barely breathe as I say, "Me too."

Jasper sighs with relief. "I'm happy to hear that, babe." He kisses the back of my hand and then my palm.

"Do we live together for a while?" I ask.

"We live together for as long as we live," he quickly says.

I grunt thoughtfully. I always believed such a heavy task would be impossible for me. "Do you think we'll last that long?"

He kisses the back of my hand again. "Baby, I'm going to put a big beautiful ring on your finger, and when I ask you to marry me, officially ask, you're going to say..." He narrows an eye, gracing me with his sexy lopsided smile as he waits for me to say something.

"I'm going to say, hell yes."

We beam at each other until he closes my computer and puts it back in the case. Jasper unfastens my seat belt and sets me on his lap. We stroke each other's erogenous zones and make out until an assortment of Chef Bart's éclairs are served. Eating the flaky and creamy desserts is akin to the orgasms Jasper had given me the previous day in his office chair. It's an honor when Chef Bart comes out of the kitchen to take a bow and thank me for being a fan.

"You really have a kitchen in your private airplane?" I ask Jasper after I hugged the chef and asked him a boatload of questions about his career as a chef.

"Wait until we travel in the luxury liner. I have a bed in that one." His eyes smolder. "I wish I had a bed in this one." Apparently, we have the same thing on our minds.

Thank goodness the captain announces that it's time to prepare for landing. Otherwise, Jasper and I would have cleared the cabin and banged each other's brains out.

TWELVE

ON THE GROUND

Nashville is just as freezing cold as Newport and Providence. I was hoping for more warmth down South. More than ever, I'm positive that I need to spend a couple of weeks on a tropical island at some point in the near future.

After landing and disembarking the private aircraft, Jasper and I quickly transfer from the aircraft to a big black SUV with tinted windows. He's sitting very close to me in the back seat, and that makes the ride extra cozy. Joe, the security guy, is driving. Jasper says we are on our way to a motel on the west end of town and off the interstate. He's worried that Bryn and Katie have put themselves in more danger than they realize. He's also very worried about Katie's partner, Zach, who is with them. Jasper blames Dale.

"Are you more worried about Zach because he's a surgical resident?" I ask.

Jasper rubs the back of his neck as if just thinking about an answer to my question troubles him. "All Arthur needs is another unsuspecting target. And given his job…"

"Right," I say, ready to pick up where he left off. "He can't so easily go into hiding."

"No." Jasper takes a long sigh. "If they'd only waited, I could have arranged a meeting with their mother in a safer location."

His cellphone dings and he glares at the screen. At first I think he's going to ignore the message from a man named Curtis Rumsfeld. But then Jasper's thumbs quickly type out a message.

I think there's a reason he's letting me see what he's writing—he's telling Curtis Rumsfeld that he isn't interested in politics and to find another candidate to prime. After hitting Send, he winks at me.

"Then it's settled," I say. "No more of this POTUS nonsense."

Grinning, he tilts his head curiously. "You mean you wouldn't have voted for me?"

I snicker. "Not when I first met you, that's for sure."

Jasper laughs heartily. I've never heard that sort of laughter from him, and because of it, I relish the sound, drinking it in, storing it in my memory bank.

"I would definitely want your vote, babe." He holds up a finger. "Even if I'd only gotten one, I would've wanted it to be yours."

I gaze at him lovingly through my eyelashes. "Well, now that I know you a lot better, I wouldn't give it to anyone else but you."

Jasper squeezes my hand tighter. "Then that would've made me a winner."

I moan as if his words were music to my ears. "You sure know how to lay it on thick. But don't stop, I love it."

Jasper chuckles. Then his gaze turns serious. "But I couldn't live under the scrutiny of being president. Not only that, but I'm not a politician. Never have been and never will be. But I know what they're made of. I've had to pay off a lot of them in my lifetime."

I grunt thoughtfully and ponder what he'd said.

"She's thinking," Jasper says.

I grin as I scratch the back of my head. *How do I say this?* "I don't think many people are like you. I mean, you can remember a sentence in a paragraph after studying the entire page for less than a minute."

"It's two minutes. And doing that is stressful."

I nod understandingly. "I can imagine it is, my love. Your father made sure you acquired that ability under a lot of duress, but you do have the ability. And I'm sure you have opinions on foreign affairs, economics, and national security."

He scoffs. "Don't we all. But I'm not interested in fixing any of it. What the hell, babe—you want me to be a president?"

I laugh. "No way," I say, shaking my head adamantly. "I just know you'd be a hell of a president if you decided to be one. I'm rather partial to the idea of you and Vincent Adams taking over the media world."

Jasper strikes again. His mouth is on mine. First his tongue plunges deep into my mouth, swirling around mine, making me moan. Then that intensity turns into pure sensual passion as his lips and tongue brush mine. It's such a delicate act. I love it this way. I feel him better—taste him better—I want him inside me.

"I love that you want me to take over the media world." His eyes smolder. "You know how much I love it?" He guides my hand to his engorged crotch. I squeeze his package. *He's as hard as steel*.

My heart skips a beat. By the way we look at each other, it's evident what we're going to do the next time we were in bed together. I still haven't taken my hand off his cock. Without even realizing it, I'm stroking him through his pants.

Jasper sucks air between his clenched teeth as he wraps his large hand around my smaller wrist. He shakes his head at me, watching me with lidded eyes. "I know you don't care who sees us, and neither do I, but we're almost at our destination, and it's time to focus."

"I understand," I whisper as our mouths slowly moved toward each other.

Then Jasper pulls back, rubbing his chin. "You're addictive."

I chuckle as I smash my finger against my chest. "Me?" I press my finger against his chest. It feels so solid, even through his sweater. "*You* are."

Jasper captures my hand and does his customary kiss to the back of it and then the palm. I beam at him, wondering if he would do that even when we're old and gray and still in love. Suddenly, my father's face came to mind. I close my eyes gravely. When he's released from jail, he will surely get in the way.

"What's that expression for?" Jasper asks.

Of course he'll ask me that question. He always notices every perceptible change in me and I notice the same with him. But I didn't want to mention Harper right now. I don't want my past to kill all the good vibes swimming around us.

"It's nothing, babe," I say. "I'm just tired."

Jasper eyes me curiously. "You should be starting your period soon?"

Finally, he's said something in front of his security guys that embarrasses the hell out of me. My face warms as I look down at the back of the front seat. "It's coming." *I hope... or maybe not.* That's a pretty stupid thought. Jasper and I have been captured by the euphoria of new love. Having a child now would not be smart. We must start using protection, and all the time.

"But I should consider some form of birth control," I say.

When I turn to him, he's watching me in that puzzled way of his.

"Are you even sure Bryn is still at the motel?" I ask in an effort to change the conversation.

That quizzical look on his face doesn't change. "She arrived forty-three minutes ago," he says in a dull tone.

I squirm in my seat. "Then you have eyes on them?" My voice is a little too excitable.

"Yes."

We're staring at each other. I wonder who's going to speak first.

"By the way, I had your father moved to a safer location."

My eyes expand so wide that he's turned blurry. I think I ask, "huh?" But I'm not certain.

He goes on to tell me that Arthur Valentine had eyes on my father, thugs who were ready to hurt him when the order was given. He says he checked into the charges and sentencing for my father. Jasper found them exorbitant for a petty criminal like Harper. That's why he had him moved to a new innovative correctional facility in Washington State where the focus is on true rehabilitation. Each prisoner has their own private space and our housed humanely. They receive psychological treatment daily and wear regular clothes.

"The concept is if they are housed and rehabilitated like humans, they will emerge a healthier citizen."

He's waiting for me to say something, but I'm speechless. *Where did this man come from? And why do I deserve him?*

"Thank you," I barely utter.

Jasper seems as if he hates he has to rip his focus off of me to take a headset from the security agent in the front passenger seat.

I force the tears that are burning my eyes back down as the vehicle pulls into the parking lot of a standard sort of motel for exhausted motorists. I've stayed in many motels like this one over the years. While on the road, chasing down stories, all I needed for lodging was a bed that could have been lumpy, hard, or too soft—I wasn't particular—and a clean toilet and shower. I never even cared if my neighbors in the rooms next to mine or below or above me were having sex so loudly that it felt as though I was an unwelcome third party. A noisy television didn't bother me, either. When I was on the road, the dirtier, dingier, and smuttier the hotel, the closer I felt I was to discovering the truth about whatever I was investigating.

This particular hotel isn't the worst of its kind, but it isn't the best, either. Our driver parks far from the building even though the parking lot wasn't that full. I noticed a satellite truck, which an odd thing to see on a day and in a place like that. Perhaps a news crew from a different city was in town and hunkering down for the rest of the day. The driver turned off the engine.

Jasper finishes putting on his headset. "Stay here."

I seize him by the arm before he can exit the back seat. "Jasper?"

He faces me.

"Are you serious?"

"Stay here. It's safer for you. I'm trying to keep you safe," he says tetchily.

"You use that word a lot—*safe*."

The men up front open their doors, and cold gusts flow in from outside.

Jasper's looking at me as if asking what more do I want him to say. To him, his decision is sound and unchallengeable. However, he isn't bullheaded, which is something I love about him. He could be persuaded, which means it's time I start persuading him.

"Jasper, I'm an investigative reporter. I want to be there for that part of myself. Understand?"

His eyes hold my gaze for a few beats. "Come on."

I stifle a sigh of relief but I can't erase my huge smile.

Jasper rubs his face. When he does that I know

he's not at all comfortable with his decision. But I also know he's not going to change his mind. His glare passes across my face and lands on his security chief. "Stay close to her, Joe."

Joe nods firmly and moves over to stand by my side.

"Let's go," Jasper says.

We start walking even though I have more questions about the logistics of his plan. But two things are true. Jasper rarely does anything without thoroughly thinking it through. And this is his operation, not mine. So I remain quiet and get a sense of everything that's going on around me just in case.

The bitterly cold air stings my face, and even my body through my coat. Picking up my pace to keep up with the long-legged men, I fold my arms and bite down hard on my back teeth to fight the shivers. Not even the brisk pace and a tight hug are enough to save me from becoming a human Popsicle. Jasper looks back in time to see me hugging myself. I can tell by his expression that he hates how miserable I appear. I smile at him gently to relieve his worry. I'm not sure if it works.

However, I'm caught off guard by the television station satellite van parked near the building.

"A news crew is here?" I ask.

"Yes," Jasper replies as he steps aside to make sure I pass him as I enter.

"Has she gone to the local news about her mother?"

"Dale," he mutters and then tells me to stay close to Joe.

The tall, fit, athletically carved man stands next to me. He has one hand on his earpiece as he looks out the glass doors. I'm already defrosted enough to keep myself from shivering. The unusual sight of the four of us immediately catches the attention of the two women behind the desk. They stare at Jasper as he strolls toward them in all his glory. Their jaws have dropped and they look at each other with eyes that ask, "Do you see what I see?"

He continues to be a sight to behold as he asks the girl with the ponytail for Beth McConnell. Her skin turns red, and she's lost for words until she coughs quickly into her balled fist. "Um, sorry. Are you with the others?"

"Do the others consist of two young women who are twins, two men, and a television crew?" Jasper asks.

Her head bobbles as she nods. Poor thing—she has been bewitched by his remarkable male beauty.

"Then yes. Where are they?" There's no softness

or charm in his tone. He's not rude, but he's definitely demanding.

"They're in the break room."

"The employees' break room?" he asks.

"Yes. I'll take you. Follow me."

I would've never gotten that far that fast
with her.

Jasper waves at us. "Let's go."

"Oh," the girl says as if she'd forgotten he isn't
alone.

Suddenly, Joe stops and presses his hand on his
earpiece. "Boss, we have eyes on subject one."

The tension between the three men is thick.

"Go," Jasper says.

Joe and the other guy bolt out the door.

The front-desk clerk is more confused about
what just happened than I am.

I trot to catch up to Jasper. "Who's subject one?"
There's a fifty-fifty chance he will answer.

"We're ready to follow," he says to the clerk.

The girl looks at me then at him like she's regret-
ting making it so easy for the good-looking guy in the
suit and says, "This way."

Jasper frowns down at me as we continue
following the front-desk clerk through a door and
down a long brightly lit hallway with dull white

linoleum floors. I look at him with raised eyebrows to let him know I'm fine and I'm not thinking of turning back now.

She stops at a closed door and turns to wiggle her eyebrows at Jasper. "They're in here."

He nods firmly at her and then looks at me. "Stay in the hallway."

Fat chance.

It must be her instincts that make her take two steps back as he walks briskly in her direction.

Jasper opens the door. "What the hell is going on?" he barks.

I'm right on his heels but I don't think he realizes that I've slipped in behind him. There are lights, cameras, and all the people operating both, along with Bryn and Katie sitting at a table across from a woman dressed in a navy-blue suit. Dale and a guy who I suppose is Zach are standing by, watching. My curious gaze lands on the small woman with deep pockmarks on her face, her eyes are red and lifeless even though she's a living human being. *Is that their mother?*

I hadn't realized I was holding my breath until the overwhelming need to breathe consumes me. Jasper quickly turns to see me. He stiffens and then turns his head slightly, chastising me. But my eyes skim his expression of disapproval and resettle on the woman sitting with Bryn and Kat.

She's so underweight that it seems that with one blow, her bones would break. She has a hacking cough too, and her front teeth are either missing or rotted. I have to stare at her for longer than usual to find the resemblance to her children. But it's definitely Beth McConnell. Her first name is embroidered on the right side of her blousy maid's shirt, which she wears with ill-fitting polyester pants.

Bryn gasps as if she just realized that Jasper is in the room. The bright lights must've blinded her.

"Jasper?" she says as she jumps to her feet.

Jasper bares his teeth. "Whatever you're doing, stop."

"It's too late," Dale says. "It's a done deal. They were live."

I've never seen Jasper look at someone like he wants to end them until this very moment.

Jasper casually looks at his face and then his death stare falls on the reporter. "You're not live. Who's your station manager? Dave Barnes?"

The reporter, a brunette about the same age as I am and probably just as ambitious is about to say something when Bryn shoots to her feet, nostrils flaring.

"Screw you, Jasper!" she yells and aims a finger at Beth. "She's my real mother." She points to Katie. "That's the sister I just met yesterday. And our father was a pedophile. Are you really determined to hide that?"

I wait for Jasper to blow a gasket and yell at everyone to clear out or else. But he swallows. He seems to be staring off into nowhere for a moment until his gaze falls on me. I know what he knows and something that Bryn doesn't know yet. I do believe if she had known that Amelia was kidnapped then she probably wouldn't be giving this interview to the local news.

"Jasper, it's too late. That was live," Bryn repeats sounding more like an adult and less like a spoiled child.

Jasper looks like he's in control but subdued. It feels as if the entire room is trapped in the eye of the storm. The technicians, reporter, boyfriends, and Jasper's sisters appear to be waiting for his next move. Finally, I massage his shoulder. He drops his gaze to my hand.

Then, suddenly, a young guy with a thin build and dots of acne who appears to be a college intern tells the reporter she has a call from Dave Barnes.

"Ah," I say silently. The earpiece Jasper is

wearing—that's why he appeared so detached from this debacle. He's been secretly and silently shifting the pieces.

"This is Sabrina," the reporter says, abruptly turning her back on us. She says, "Uh-huh," several times and then, "But... Got it."

Sabrina ends the call. When she looks at Jasper there is no sign that she's effected by his beauty and allure. Inhaling nasally, Sabrina pulls her shoulders back as she beams in on Jasper. "We have to pack up. But, the interview is complete. I've been told to ask if you would like to see it."

THIRTEEN
NEXT STOP
HOLLY HENDERSON

We're sitting and watching the interview. Jasper's body is tight, his jaw is tight too, and I'm feeling what he's feeling. Bryn has left no stone unturned. She and Katie are on camera talking about the moment they met and how it was to see each other for the first time. Sabrina Lowland, the reporter for the local station, wouldn't have been worth her salt if she hadn't gotten right to the point, which was the reason why this particular story was so important. She gave a brief biography of the late Randolph Blackstone, including all his achievements in business and politics.

"But you're saying there was a different person behind the mask?" Sabrina asks.

Bryn's face tightens, pinched by pure hate. "He was more like a monster."

Her ominous tone squeezes my heart.

And then Sabrina Lowland continues to conduct an interview worthy of a Peabody Award. Bryn speaks of her relationship with her father, citing an incident when she was a young girl and how he had fondled her. She says he would have done more to her if it weren't for her brother, Jasper, who always kept her safe.

"That was his job, protecting all of us from our father."

I catch Bryn as she averts her gaze to Jasper, but he does not look at her. He's pissed that this interview even exists. I think after watching this interview, and with all the people who heard Bryn make her claims, there's no putting this Genie back in the box. Jasper knows it, and that's why he's fuming.

On the television monitor, Sabrina, who's a shark lapping up the blood in the water, continues taking large bites out of her kill. She asks a leading question regarding Katie's similar experience with their father, and that's when the most damaging part of the interview occurs. Katie speaks about the house she grew up in. Jasper rounds his shoulders back twice as if he's trying to take the tension out of them as Beth, their mother, who's right by Katie's side, looking battered by life, confirms that she had only been fourteen years old when the old man had sex with her. By way of Sabrina's careful guidance, Beth and Katie share traumatic details about the lives they lived inside the house in Chattanooga. The numb, unfeeling way that they relive those moments chills me to the bone. I thought I had it bad with my parents, but not really. Even with their weaknesses they protected me. Beth, who hasn't spoken as much as Katie has, says she ran away from an abusive home when she was twelve years old to only end up at another one.

"But they would get into your head and brain-wash you, I guess," Beth says. Her voice is gruff like someone who has smoked too many cigarettes or burned out her vocal cords smoking hard drugs.

"When did you leave the house in Chattanooga?" Sabrina asks.

"After Katie, escaped. There was no need to be there no more," Beth replies.

Suddenly, and shocking everyone, Katie wails into her palms. Her shoulders jerk convulsively. The camera stays on her and drives in for a closeup, exploiting her breakdown. They're shameless. The cameras capture Zach, as he sits beside her and puts his arm around her. Katie rests her face on his chest and continues crying as he presses his lips against the top of her head.

"You were the one who saved her?" Sabrina asks Zach.

Zach scowls at Sabrina. "Come on, baby," he whispers lovingly as he guides Katie to her feet and walks her out of the camera's view.

Jasper rips his attention off the screen to nod at Zach in appreciation. Zach nods back. I search over my right shoulder looking for Dale to see how he's reacting to the interview. He's not where he was last standing. I search across my left shoulder. He's not there either. *Has he slipped out?*

The interview continues, and by now, watching just feels painful. Sabrina makes a comment about how tragic and painful their story is, "as we can see." She then asks Bryn when did she learn that Amelia Blackstone wasn't her mother. Jasper rubs the side of his face. The Bryn on camera looks as if she's second-guessing her decision to be part of the interview but she now realizes that it's too late to turn back.

"Did you know that the authorities are looking into a claim that Amelia Blackstone was kidnapped?" Sabrina asks.

"How the fuck..." Jasper mutters as he squeezes the back of his head. "Stop it."

Bryn on camera stares at Sabrina like she's watching an oncoming car about to slam into her and it's too late to get out of the way.

The monitor cuts off. Jasper glares at Bryn as if to say, "You don't know what you have done." And her watery eyes are trained on him like she's very much aware that she knows she screwed up.

———

JASPER CLEARS the crew out of the room, including Sabrina Lowland. I think Sabrina already knows that her interview will be wiped before they make it back to the station. There is someone Jasper is speaking to who's doing his dirty work. For instance, as Sabrina's crew walked out of the room, Joe called each of them to a private location to do only God knows what. I'll have to ask Jasper later. Now, the only people who are left are the Blackstone family and their close contacts. Arms folded, hugging herself tight, Bryn stares at the door as if she just realizes Dale is no longer with us.

"He's gone," Jasper says to her.

She nods.

And then Jasper steps completely into take charge mode.

He composedly turns to Beth and says her name.

She's shivering under his focused glare. I think his energy and the fact that he's a Blackstone male scares her. "Um, yeah?" she says and then hacks into her fist.

"Are you currently using drugs?" Jasper's tone is like that of a doctor.

"No," she says, sounding like a little kid who's lying about doing something wrong.

Jasper of course doesn't believe her which is why he asks, "Are you open to drug-abuse rehabilitation?"

"I've been sober for six months," she says with a nod. It's evident she wants to convince Jasper that she isn't a druggie anymore. "I lived a long time on the streets. But now I have this job, and it pays me enough to keep a place where I'm warm, and I have some food in the refrigerator too." She sounds proud of herself.

Jasper's expression hasn't change. "I understand. But, are you willing to enter a proper rehabilitation center?"

Beth's brows ruffle and then evens out as her eyes dart around in her sockets.

"It'll be one of the best rehabilitation facilities in

the country," he says as if he's hoping to help her make her decision. "It'll work if you go into it, wanting it to work."

"Beth," Bryn's voice breaks the pensive silence. "I think you should. I'll go with you." She sounds vulnerable, pleading.

Beth looks from one of her daughters to the other. "The boy," she says to Jasper.

"Asher," Bryn says.

"Was he? Is he?"

"He's fine," Jasper says.

"He was raised with me," Bryn follows up.

Beth closes her eyes as she swallows hard. She drops her head. "I'll go."

AS JASPER GUESSED, Zach wouldn't fly back to the compound for safe keeping. He had to return to his long shifts at the hospital. So Jasper had flown him on a private flight back to New York City and insisted that Zach stay in his apartment in Manhattan, where he would be kept under guard. Zach didn't want any special treatment, but Jasper convinced him to take up residence at the apartment by explaining that as long as Katie loved him, he could be a target of a soulless man due to a long-standing war between families that would be ending soon.

However, Zach agreed to stay at the apartment under one condition. "Katie remains under guard with me."

Bryn gasped with shock as her and Katie's eyes met. They hadn't known each other that long and they were already practicing twin-telepathy.

"After I fly with Beth to California," Bryn said, "I'll join the two of you at the apartment."

I can tell that Jasper was relieved that there was no talk of Dale. After this episode, I can see why Jasper has always been hellbent on keeping that man as far away as possible from Bryn. But at least, a plan is made that Jasper could get onboard with.

---

3 Hours Later

Jasper and I make one more stop before securing ourselves in the luxurious compound where Jasper promises we will finally relax, make love, and eat a lot of Chef Bart's food. It's taken three hours to fly from Nashville to Charleston, West Virginia. Amelia

Blackstone's kidnapping has already been leaked to certain media outlets, including BCN. During the flight Jasper was on the phone with David Eastman and Vincent Adams, both men letting him know that BCN must absolutely break the story in a big and comprehensive way to save face. Their call was on speaker so that I could hear and perhaps lend some advice.

But I didn't need to add an opinion at all. Jasper had come up with the most effective decision on his own. First, we meet his grandparents, and then tomorrow morning at 7:00 p.m. EST, Jasper will appear on the Stan Rochester Show, BCN's highest rating nightly news show, as a special guest. Teaser packages, announcing his guest appearance are already being produced.

Then, Jasper let me grill him like a good investigative reporter. I asked him the tough questions.

"How long have you known about your father's tendency to exploit underage girls?" I had asked.

Jasper looked me dead in the eye and said, "The answer to you, Holly, is that I have known since Gina was introduced to our family. I cannot break her confidence and tell you her story but she was very young when her existence came to my attention."

I swallowed to moisten my dry throat. I could

hardly believe what I was hearing. "And you just let him continue," I asked, frowning as a bitter taste filled my mouth.

"No. I fought him every step of the way."

"Short of turning him in," I say with a snarl.

"No. I didn't. I couldn't." Jasper shakes his head. "Stopping him was not so cut and dry, Holly. You should know this. I had to stop one incident at a time, one girl at a time. I never told anybody this, but I am telling you this."

His eyebrows furrow as a distant glint enters his eyes. He tells me about the day his father suffered his first major stroke. Jasper had informed him that he had arranged a takeover of BFE by way of securing proxy votes from ninety-three percent of the board.

"Wow," I mouthed. "I'd never heard of one person landing ninety-three percent of the vote. How did you manage that?"

It was as if the memory had made Jasper's neck feel stiff so he stretched it from one side to the other. "I raided their closets, collected their skeletons, and then showed them the bones." He watched me with raised eyebrows, waiting to see if I understood his analogy.

A chill came over me as I nodded and folded my arms. "What are you going to do with those bones?"

"The bones are why this entire situation has turned very dangerous, Holly. The leaks could send a lot of bad people running. But I have a guy, Nestor. He's on it."

I narrowed an eye. "Nestor?"

"What happened at the motel—that was him."

I really applauded Jasper for saying so much without really giving much away at all. He finally confirmed that after Randolph had heard that his CEO days were over and he was no longer in charge of the family enterprise, he literally got so angry, so worked up, that his brain blew a gasket and he suffered his first major stroke.

"Going back to my initial question—what will you say to Stan Rochester tomorrow?" I had asked.

"I uncovered my father's lewd deeds after he fell ill and I was able to uncover his secrets."

"How?" I rapid fired.

"I gained access to records and recordings. I was able to find all that was hidden."

My face remained as emotionless as a stone. "Why did you look?"

"Because he was never a good man, Stan. I have never been recorded, saying that he was. As a matter of fact, I staged a successful coup to take over BFE before my father fell ill. After which, I uncovered a long history of sexual harassment and just plain old sexual battery. The evidence has already been turned over to the FBI."

After a swift intake of air, I ask, "Are you bull-shitting, Stan?"

Jasper shook his head swiftly and said, "No. Heads will roll, very soon."

I nodded approvingly and then said, "You're good."

He smirked and said, "So are you."

Then, the pilot announced that we were land-ing, and now it's early in the evening and Jasper and I in a rental car roll to a stop in front of a white house.

"Here we are," he barely says, leaning forward to get an eyeful of the house his grandparents live in. They're expecting us.

I also turn to study the grayish-blue classic craftsman home. Warm light glows along the edge of the curtains, covering large square windows, one on each side of the door. The yard is covered with snow and the trees around the perimeter have been beaten by the cold spell that's befallen the country this winter. However, I can tell that when spring arrives, their branches would sprout healthy green leaves. Then, my eyes, fall on a charming mailbox made like an old tree house and has the name Hollander engraved on the front.

"This is it." Jasper's voice cracks a little.

"Yep," I say with a yawn, still studying the scale of the property Jasper's grandparents have made for themselves, trying to assess what sort of people they were.

Jasper reaches out to take my hand. "I'm glad you're here with me, but if you prefer to rest, we can check in to a hotel and come back tomorrow morning."

I'm worn out, that's for sure, but there's no way we can delay this meeting. Plus, we're embarking on a significant piece of the puzzle to the mystery of Amelia Blackstone's past. My body is tired, but the investigative journalist in me has the stamina of a superhero.

I squeeze Jasper's hand. "I'm fine, my love. We're here now, so let's not drag out the inevitable. Plus, I'm too curious. There's no way I'll be able to sleep tonight."

I turn to Jasper who arches his thick and well-kept eyebrows. "I'm not planning on you getting much sleep tonight."

I smile sheepishly as I stifle another yawn. Jasper reaches out to delicately cup the side of my face.

Gazing into his eyes helps with my tiredness. Then his lips softly brush mine and our tongues join in.

"Mm..." we both say, restraining ourselves from extending our kiss.

My eyes flutter open as the remains of our kiss slowly dissipates. "Marie and Harold, right?"

"Yes," he whisper breathily.

I nod.

After taking a deep breath, Jasper opens his door. "Stay seated." He gets out of our comfy car to retrieve our coats out of the trunk and then opens my door. Jasper, quickly helps me into my coat, and together, holding hands, we walk up the driveway. I'm not sure if Jasper knows how tightly he's gripping my hand. We make it to the porch, and without taking a moment to collect himself, Jasper rings the doorbell.

FOURTEEN

TO THE GRANDS

A tall, slender man wearing casual pants and a thick navy-blue cable-knit sweater stood in front of us. He asks who we are, and Jasper gives him the name of his contact at the FBI. Harold Hollander opens the door immediately.

The two men, grandson and grandfather, study each other. The moment feels very odd. Harold, who is quite handsome with his piercing light eyes, supple lips, and hair grayed at the temples of his angular face, studies Jasper with his mouth agape. It must be very odd for him to look at his grandson and perhaps see a carbon copy of himself from at least thirty years ago. They're the same height. Even though Harold is thinner and lacking Jasper's athletic frame, they have the same physique.

"Who are you?" Harold asks. The question seems to escape him involuntarily. He clears his throat.

"Who is it, Harry?" a woman, who I presume is Marie, calls from within the bowels of the house. She's close, and I can hear her footfalls as she moves closer.

Then a beautiful woman with piercing eyes, a swan's neck, and long lean arms, legs and torso arrives to stand by her husband's side. There is no doubt that she is Jasper's grandmother, Marie. The woman appears awestricken as one of her hands seems to involuntarily rise to cover her mouth.

Jasper peers at them both as if he's having no emotional reaction to them at all. "I'm Jasper Walker Blackstone."

Harold frowns as if he's chewing on a lemon. "Blackstone?"

"Yes. I'm Amelia Blackstone's son. You may know her as Doris Hollander. Your daughter." Again, he sounds like an emotionless robot.

However, Marie, who has not yet taken her hand off her mouth, shoulders curve over as she sobs into her palms.

THE INTERIOR OF THE HOLLANDERS' home resembles that of people my parents used to take advantage of. Trinkets are carefully put on shelves sharing space with framed photos of young kids and adults, all having unique renditions of Jasper and his grandfather's gorgeous eyes. The fact that the couple apparently went on to have more children, puts what feels like a boulder in my chest. I'm certain Jasper feels this way too, although he's not showing it.

After the photo tour where we've learned the names of many of Jasper's uncles, aunts, nieces, nephews, and cousins, we all sit at a table in a very tight dining room. I take note of the china cabinet filled with rows of glasses and stacked plates. I wonder if Marie and Harold ever use them. An antique crystal chandelier in the art deco style hangs over the wood stained table. This space, this house, feels like a grandparent's home.

Harold talks about how he and Marie reacted after hearing of his existence. I'm worried about Jasper's stoic demeanor. He's not your ordinary human being. He's like a gladiator in the world of mere men. In a sense, that was what his sick father had striven to make him.

Small talk continues as the air is thick with a conversation that must be had. Marie gets up to make coffee, and it seems that Harold cannot take his eyes off Jasper.

"Are the two of you married?" Harold asks Jasper.

"Not yet," Jasper replies. "Soon."

My eyebrows shoot up. Soon? That's news to me. The thing is... I want to marry Jasper soon. I wanted to be married to him five minutes ago, and then five minutes before that, and so on and so on.

Harold glances at Marie as if all the superficial pleasantries are over and he's looking for her to join him to provide support of what is sure to be a difficult conversation to come.

"My father's name is Randolph Blackstone. Have you ever heard of him?" Jasper asks.

Harold's eyebrows ruffle and then releases. I sense that he does know Randolph but doesn't want to acknowledge it.

"Randolph Blackstone of Blackstone Family Enterprise," Jasper continues as if he has to provide more clues.

Marie sits down close to her husband and links arms with him as the coffee brews.

"I didn't know him personally, but I know of him." Harold turns to his wife, who keeps shaking her head. "We found out yesterday that he..." Harold clears his throat as Marie squeezes his arm tighter. "He had Doris."

Jasper's eyes narrow to slits. "You didn't know?"

Harold jerks his head back and then stares angrily at his grandson. "No, I did not know. If I knew where my daughter was, I would've called the authorities. And if I knew that man had my daughter"—he pounds the table with the tip of his finger—"I would've killed him with my bare hands."

Jasper looks at me, puzzled, and then reaches into his coat pocket and takes out his mother's diary. "I want to read you something."

I hide my surprise. I didn't know Jasper had brought the diary. He starts reading what he'd read to me this morning, the part where Amelia or Doris accuses her parents of being paid off by Randolph Blackstone.

"That never happened," Harold appears very disturbed by what he just heard.

I touch Jasper's arm, signaling to him that I have something to say. "Could you tell us what happened on the day your daughter went missing?"

"Yes," Marie says, gazing at the table as she nods. "After school, Doris went to a friend's house and never came home. The girl's name was Penelope Donaldson. She said..."

"It was the ceremony, honey," Harold says, cutting her off as if he just remembered something.

Marie watches with a distraught frown. "The ceremony?"

His eyes turn down at the corners as he looks at Jasper. "I'm a retired scientist. At the time of Doris's disappearance, I was working for United Alliance Laboratories Chemicals."

"That's one of ours," Jasper says as if he just found a significant piece to the puzzle.

Harold's brows furrow and even out as he studies his grandson. "I created a chemical compound that UALC purchased from me."

"You're paid a royalty fee," Jasper says.

Harold squeezes his eyes closed like he's trying to banish tears and perhaps stop himself from throwing up. "For years," he's only barely able to say.

We let silence reign as Marie rubs the top part of Harold's back as his shoulder's shake.

Jasper and I steal a knowing glance at each other. Randolph must've shown Amelia the royalty checks and proof that he bought her from her parents. And that is a particularly evil, no diabolical, thing to do.

Finally, Harold is composed enough to tell Jasper the name of the chemical agent he had created and what it was used for. "We had a ceremony for my achievement. I brought my family. My daughter and your father were both there." Harold turns to his wife. "I mentioned how I didn't like the way he looked at her. Do you remember that, Marie?"

"I remember it," Marie says sadly. "I didn't take you seriously. I called you crazy, but you were right." Her voice cracks.

"The next week, she went missing," Harold says.

Jasper cocks his head. "I remember reading about that patent. It was returned to you in full six years ago."

Harold nods stiffly. "I never knew why. It didn't make sense. If only I had..." He presses his lips tightly. "I just didn't expect a man like him to do something like that."

Jasper takes my hand under the table. "I have to tell you about my father and the sort of man he was. You're going to hear about it in the news, and I want you to hear it from me first."

———

Half An Hour Later

Marie sits very still as tears roll down her cheeks. She doesn't swipe them—she lets them paint her skin

with wetness. At that moment, I can feel how much
sadness they are experiencing about the loss and life
of their daughter. They are deathly silent when
Jasper makes it to the hardest part and tells them
about how Randolph Blackstone had preferred girls
of a certain age and, because of his massive wealth,
could afford to not only feed his sickness but also
keep it secret. Jasper tells them his mother was fourteen years old when she birthed him. He shares with
them how their daughter boldly chose to stay with
Randolph because of him.

"She wanted me to end him. To take everything
he had and leave him with nothing. I was just begin-
ning the process when Randolph fell ill."

There's a bitter look on Jasper's face, one formed
by pure hate, perhaps it's a projection of Doris's
hate.

Marie and Harold share a look. It seems as if
they don't know how to respond to what they just
heard.

"But Randolph was a master manipulator,"
Jasper continues. "I'm positive he convinced my
mother that you let him have her."

Then Jasper let them know what childhood
he had.

Harold clears his throat. "We never left this

house because we hoped one day Doris would return."

Marie shakes her head vigorously. "I never believed she was dead. I knew someone had her. I would stare at men, wishing they would see something in my face to tip me off that they had her. I didn't care what they did to her. I wouldn't even turn them in, I just wanted her back." Face still wet, tears continuously rolling, Marie gazes off unfocused and repeats, "I just wanted her back."

Harold guides his wife against him. Marie lays her head on his shoulder and he kisses her forehead, letting his lips linger on her forehead for a few beats. They are a strikingly beautiful older couple in their late sixties. Their pain is evident though. It's the sort that could knock a human being to the ground and make it hard to stand back up.

"But you stayed to fight him?" Harold asks, his watery eyes begging to hear more about the strength of his daughter.

"Yes," Jasper replies. "And I won. We won."

Harold nods as though hearing that is some consolation for losing his beautiful daughter. He presses his cheek against his wife's forehead. "Hear that honey? Doris was still tough. The way you taught her to be."

"Yes she..." Marie cries as her entire body shakes as she sobs uncontrollably.

AFTER JASPER'S grandmother wipes her tears, I help Marie serve the coffee. They invite us to stay with them for the night, and Jasper and I accept their invitation. Marie and Harold show us tons of photos of Doris when she was a little girl and of their other children. They want Jasper to meet them soon. Jasper seems hesitant but eventually says he would like that.

Jasper tells them that his mother was a pretty good photographer and liked taking pictures. He says he had some of her photos framed on his walls in all his homes. Marie excuses herself and returns with a tiny camera that her daughter used to keep on her most of the time.

"She'd always be out taking pictures. I have her photo album somewhere around here."

Unable to restrain myself, I yawn, and Harold asks his wife if we could save that part for the morning.

THEY SHOW Jasper and me to a guest room, which has a queen-sized bed and antique furniture and smells of potpourri. Thankfully, there's an attached bathroom which has an old-fashioned clawfoot shower tub combo.

"I bet you have never slept in a queen-sized bed," I say to Jasper as I strip out of my jeans and sweater.

Jasper snorts a cynical chuckle as he takes off his underwear. "Take it all off," he says, pointing to my panties and bra. And then he climbs into the small bed.

I eye him suspiciously as I strip out of my underwear, and get in bed with him. *I'm sure he's not planning on fucking in his grandparent's house.*

I raise my body to look down at the foot of the bed. "Are your feet hanging over?"

Jasper draws me against him and I snuggle against his hard body.

"Yes, but I'm fine," he says grinding me with an erection the size of Jupiter.

"Do you really think we should, with Ward and June down the hall?" I whisper.

"Who are Ward and June?"

I chuckle. "You know, the Cleavers—*Leave It to Beaver.*"

"Is that a book?" His breath tickles the back of my neck.

"No, it's a television show."

He grunts thoughtfully as his large, soft hands cup my breasts and kneads them. "I don't know about those two Cleavers, but..." The tip of his boss pokes the outside of my sex.

Sighing, feeling pleasure, I open my legs a little wider and let him move inside me.

"Um," I say.

"Damn, baby," Jasper whispers, his mouth against my hair as he shifts his manhood in and out of me. I'm so thankful the bed doesn't creak. "You're so wet, baby," he sighs.

"Jasper... um... they're going to hear us." Damn it. He feels so good inside me. I lick my lips.

"How many kids have they had? They've had a lot of sex in their lifetime." He grabs my hips, sucking air.

I twist my body to see him, watching his cock glide in and out of me.

"Your ass is famous, baby."

I chuckle. Usually, by now, Jasper would be so turned-on that he would increase his pace, but he's being careful. He cares whether his grandparents hear us. Then, he slams his cock deep inside me and presses his hand against my belly as he shivers while coming, being way more quiet than usual.

As our breathing and vitals even out, we talk about our conversation with Marie and Harold. He tells me all the thoughts he was having that I wanted so desperately to know. He says they feel like his family. He also feels as if he's known them for all his life. It's odd because he knows he hasn't though. It also hurt him terribly whenever Marie cried. She still hasn't quite come to grips with his mother's death.

"Will you take Harold and Marie to your mother's gravesite?" I ask and then yawn. Her ashes are buried on the Blackstone estate.

Jasper kisses me softly on my bare shoulder. "If they ask, yes. Get some sleep, baby."

"Okay," I say with another yawn. I'm so wiped.

Jasper is still inside me when I transition into full-fledged sleep. Sometime during the night, I woke up to pee. In the morning, I woke to the feeling of Jasper massaging my hip.

I moan. "Good morning, my love," I whisper.

He guides me onto my back and parts my thighs as he positioned himself on top of me. "Good morning."

I sigh as his cock fills me.

WE HAVE breakfast with his grandparents. Jasper and I share a quick and astonished look when they ask to see the home where Amelia was kept. Jasper agrees to show them the mansion Amelia had lived in.

"And where was she buried?" Harold asks. He readjusts in his seat like asking that question has made him very uncomfortable.

Jasper tells him that she's on the property. She had been cremated.

"We'd like to have her here. We have a family plot," Marie says. "And of course we'll make space for you." Her voice cracks and she swallows.

Jasper tells them more about their daughter. He will take them to speak to those who knew Doris best like Sally Preacher and even Nigel. Jasper even reveals that Amelia and Nigel had been in love until the day she died.

Marie's frown is severe as her gaze holds Jasper's. "How did she die?"

Jasper tells them how cancer had spread through Amelia's body. It happened so fast and she refused treatment.

After looking through the photo albums Marie

wanted to show us last night, Jasper becomes less hesitant about meeting his mother's siblings and his cousins sometime in the near future.

It's early afternoon when Jasper announces that we have to get going. He preps them for his interview on the Stan Rochester Show this evening. They should watch.

"We will," Harold says as they walk us to the door. He warns us to watch our step. "I'm going to have to shovel that walk later. The guy who takes care of our yard has been sick for the last two weeks. The flu's going around."

"I'll shovel it before we go," Jasper says. "And then I'll find you someone more stable to do your yard work for you."

I knew it wouldn't be long before Jasper started taking care of them too. I'm surprised he hasn't insisted they return to the compound with us.

Harold pats his grandson on the shoulder. "I know you're a very rich man, but so am I. How about we shovel together?"

MARIE and I watched Jasper and Harold shovel together. They were never lost for words. I told

Marie that I loved seeing a smile on Jasper's face. He's not generally a smiler.

"Neither is Harold," Marie revealed.

We shared all sorts of things that Harold and Jasper have in common. They both rub the side of their faces when they're anxious about something. They both have a propensity to want to save the world and fiercely protect those they love. And there's something else.

Before getting in the car, we turn back to wave at Harold and Marie, who are standing in the window, waving at us. The engine is already running and the car is already heated when we get in.

"Well," I say, amused by how content Jasper looks, "that was fun."

He smiles tightly, then his expression turned serious. "Holly?"

"Wait," I say, remembering what I've been so desperately wanting to tell him.

Jasper raises eyebrows in alarm and curiosity.

"Your grandfather also has the ability to remember what he reads."

After he picks his jaw up off the floor he asks, "What?"

"Yeah," I say smiling. "Your grandmother told me."

He pulls the corners of his mouth downward and grunts thoughtfully. "Interesting."

"I thought so."

"And babe, all hell's about to break loose. Our family's secrets are going to cause a ruckus. I know you said that you don't like writing, but I would like for you to write our story."

My brain can hardly connect with what he just said. "Our story? Yours and mine?"

"I'm sure that'll be included—you are the woman I love. But I'm referring to my father, mother—everything. You'll use my mother's diary as a guide. I read it from cover to cover." Jasper rubs the side of his face. "I don't want you to leave any stone unturned. All of it—I want all of it out."

I close my mouth, swallow, and eye him suspiciously. "Is this you attempting to control the narrative?"

Jasper's serious expression doesn't falter. "No. I want you to write about the Blackstones as you wrote about the Howsleys. Do what you have to do to win another prize."

He's grinning at me in his sexy way. My heart is pounding so hard. I can't speak, I'm so elated, so motivated. All I can do is nod. Then I scramble for my purse.

"What are you doing?" he asks.

"Emailing my publisher." I grin from ear to ear. "I'm telling him I have another winning story."

I glance up at Jasper and then do a double take. He looks slightly worried for a moment, but that expression quickly gives way to a smile of approval. Then he pulls the car away from the curb, and we are on our way.

FIFTEEN

I'M A BLACKSTONE
HOLLY HENDERSON

December 22nd

Another year is on the verge of being deposited in the bank of time. The publisher had rushed my new book, *The Dark Blackstones*, to print. It was touted as my best work yet—so well written, so thorough, and showing much maturity since the publication of *The Howsley Project*.

Jasper and I are now living together in his three-story penthouse apartment in New York with Katie and Zach, who were ironically married on Valentine's Day. There is more than enough room for the four of us. She's studying biology at NYU, and passing all her classes with flying colors, which isn't a surprise since she's always studying. Zach is still the second-hardest-working man I know, slaving away as a resident at the hospital. But Jasper still takes the prize for working the most. The fallout from my book exposing the secrets of the Blackstones has broken up the core family members. We don't know where Asher or Spencer are. And Bryn had eventually followed Dale to Los Angeles and suffered a mental breakdown. She's in recovery so she can't be here tonight either. In the book, Jasper didn't let me shy away from the controversy. He let me disclose all his father's dirty secrets, from the kidnapping of Doris to having children with very young girls to the extreme sexual misconduct that had taken place for years in the Lower Manhattan office. He also discovered all the aliases his father used to do his dirty deeds which included one of the names that Kylie had given to me a year ago, while I was at the Blackstone mansion. One name was Benjamin Dow. I had taken note that she had indeed passed real sources to me in relation to the Blackstones. She really wanted me to take the family down.

Arthur Valentine's power has been completely neutralized. He is broke and without money he's unable to pay bad people to do his dirty work. I heard that Julia is attempting to marry a fifth cousin to recover a tiny amount of their former wealth. I think Jasper had his hands in stopping that merger between the Valentines as well.

Yesterday morning, Jasper and I boarded his private jet and flew to where we are now. It's his own private island in the Bahamas. We had disappointed our families when right after the Stan Rochester Report taped Jasper's exclusive interview back in February, he and I flew to California and had a quick two person wedding on the private beach of his Malibu home. It has been wonderful being Mrs. Jasper Blackstone. He is the best husband a woman could ever ask for. So this Christmas, not only am I a Blackstone, but Jasper and I are hosting the Hollanders and my father, who has been surprisingly rehabilitated, for a one week resort holiday here at the wonderful estate which has a main house and twelve private luxury cabanas surrounding a sparkling and fun pool. We're expecting at least fifty people. But we're not running around like chickens with our heads cut off because Jasper has paid a lot of people to do that for us.

But today, belongs to me and Jasper. I'm standing on the block cement steps that leads to a pristine white sand beach. I drink in the sight of Jasper stretched out on a chaise lounge, hands stacked behind his head, perhaps staring at the green mountains of the mainland across the bright blue sea or maybe his eyes are closed and he's given into the gentle roll and release of the soft waves, the mild rumble of the sea, the warm fresh air, and has been lulled to sleep.

Finally, my cellphone chimes and I quickly answer the call.

"Kylie," I say. We've planned this call. It's about time we officially had it out.

"What?" she snaps.

I shake my head rapidly as I narrow an eye. "I heard you've been wanting to talk to me."

"I heard you ruined my career," she bites back.

"You ruined your own career by trying to steal my story."

"He made you do that? Your husband?"

My husband... I love the sound of that.

"No. I just wanted to get you off my back and wow, like, what kind of reporter writes up an article and not check her sources?"

Kylie's silent for a few beats. I think she's taping our call. "You and I are officially over. And you better watch your back. You're married to a criminal and I'll catch him, and you too." She ends our call.

I pull my cellphone away from my ear and look at the screen. Wow, she actually ended our call. I grunt musingly and then skip down the rest of the steps and run across the warm loose sand, my feet getting buried with each step.

When I make it to the chaise lounge set beside Jasper, he turns to smile at me. So he's not asleep. He stretches an arm for me to take his hand; I gladly take it.

"You were right," I say as I lay back and wait for the sun to set.

"You spoke with Kylie?"

"Yeah." I sigh.

"And you offered her the job?"

"She didn't even let me. She called you a criminal and said we better watch our backs."

Jasper laughs and I'm surprised his eyebrows hadn't come crashing down into a severe frown instead. I had felt bad for setting her up. Since Jasper and Vincent Adams run BCN, I asked if he would let me offer her a job on the Rochester Report, Rachel's show has been cancelled. She just couldn't allow herself to work for the new regime.

"I see you're not taking her threat serious."

"Babe, she steals stories for a living—so, no. Come..." he says, drawing me to him.

Oh, forgot to mention—we're naked.

Jasper's gaze is hooded as I lock eyes with him,

straddling him. There's no better thing to make me forget about Kylie and her threat than Jasper's ready cock. We have a lot of sex. I thought we would slow down by now but we haven't. He holds his engorged cock steady as I slowly lower myself on top of it. I toss my head back, sighing as I feel him moving inside me.

"Yes, baby, I..." he whispers before his mouth consumes my right breast.

I moan, shifting against his cock and then...

Well...

You know the rest.

SIXTEEN

EPILOGUE
SPENCER BLACKSTONE

I changed after my father died. Not because the old man wasn't around to remind me of how useless I am either. I suffered a renewal of some sort. My heart, mind, and all organs in my body felt regenerated. I didn't see it as a good thing, though. I found the change to be inevitable. I also drank too much. I would look in the mirror and punch my reflection, shattering the glass, cutting my fist. Then, I decided to read my sister-in-law's biography about my family. *Who in the hell told her all of that shit about me?* It couldn't have been Jasper. She knew things I never told him. I couldn't believe my brother co-signed on that damn book.

I saw myself in those pages as a man I never wanted to become. For weeks after I finished the book, I drank a lot more than before while wallowing in self-pity. Determined I was a decrepit asshole, I swore off women. I wasn't fit for love. At least that's what I thought. Then one night, drunk and contemplating ending it all, I remembered something about a woman I'd never met—my birth mother. That's when I set out to find her, dead or alive.

This decision invigorated me. I followed a promising lead that took me to an abandoned ranch in Wyoming. I lived there for a while, isolated. Finally, I was starting to make some progress.

But I needed to hire help, someone who could keep their whereabouts and mine confidential. It was sheer luck that Jada Forte's resume came to my attention. I knew her mother well. Any daughter of Patricia Forte should know how to keep the door to the closet which houses skeletons closed and locked.

I hired Patricia's daughter. And then I met her. One look and Jada took my breath away. Now she's in my house, stirring parts of me that have been dormant. Can I avoid her? If so, then for how long?

Read Spencer's story, start with Enthrall book one.

ABOUT THE AUTHOR

Z.L. has been writing romance full-time since 2011, which has allowed her to amass quite a catalog of romance novels. She loves what she does, and as she's evolved, so have her stories. Now, she's focused on writing angsty, sensual, and emotionally deep romance where characters have reached the point in life where they are ready for true and lasting love.

When Z.L.'s not writing, she loves to cook and read good books, which have the power to take her somewhere she's never been.

For more information:
zlarkadiebooks.com
contact@zlarkadiebooks.com

Printed in Great Britain
by Amazon

35977962R00116